REPAIRABLE MEN

# REPAIRABLE MEN

## A SHORT STORY COLLECTION

## JOHN CARR WALKER

sunnyoutside
Buffalo

ISBN: 978-1-934513-47-7

Library of Congress Control Number: 2014954432

© 2014 John Carr Walker

Cover and Book Design by Stewart A. Williams

sunnyoutside
PO Box 911
Buffalo, NY 14207
USA
www.sunnyoutside.com

*For Trish and Sam*

# REPAIRABLE MEN

A man who knew me well said that I was more innocent than any adult had the right to be. As if I had chosen to be naïve. Besides, the fact is that even extremely naïve people know their own interests.

–*Ravelstein*, Saul Bellow, 2000.

# AIN'T IT PRETTY

Marbles is a dropkick dog. A Pomeranian football. It nests inside my coat, a snarl laced into pink gums. Every old woman and little kid at the Amtrak station tries to pet it, tousling its ears and laughing at its bared needle teeth, but none of them share my history with this evil little dog.

Marbles, my mother's third and last pride and joy, should have been buried with her. I bet my brother Reg that within six months of her passing, Marbles would slip into the sweet hereafter—I lost that bet a year ago. Now my patience with toweling up raisin-sized turds and keeping its bowl filled with expensive kibble has come to an end. Reg is coming home. He's the reason I'm standing in the rain, a dog head barking from the open vee of my coat, waiting for a train that's running hours late. Reg: the disloyal son, the Stone brother with no conscience. I need his help.

He arrives at four o'clock (on the noon train), steps from the coach with a knapsack over his shoulder and a John Deere hat perched atop his head. His frown twists when he sees me, not into a smile. He's never had a good face for hats.

"Mr. Stone," he says, shaking my hand. "What's with the mongrel baby?"

"Let's get your bags," I say.

He punches the knapsack. "All I need, big brother."

In my truck he sheds his denim coat. I lift Marbles from its cocoon and place it in the blanket-lined basket on the floorboard. "Leave it alone during a storm," I say, "and you come back to chewed table legs and disemboweled couch cushions and big, black puddles of pee on the carpet."

"That's to be expected in the spawn of Satan." Reg floats two fingers at Marbles, *Three Stooges*–style. It growls, nips. "Why don't Danielle and Nicky dog-sit?" he says.

"No tormenting. It'll leap for your jugular."

Reg sits with his legs around the knapsack and drums the top. He watches the scenery absently, I think, for a man who hasn't been home in two years. He lifts and settles the hat and I catch a glimpse of the hair loss he's complained about. Last time home, two years ago, he told me, "Your little brother's growing up to be a bald man," but his hair was braided and reached past his shoulder blades and there wasn't so much as a part line showing his scalp.

The train crosses the street behind us and Reg flips it off with both barrels. "Two birds by one Stone," he says. Our old joke.

On the freeway the storm turns violent, the sky black, cracked with lightning. I hit the wipers, but the rain's as thick as gel on the windshield. I sit forward, arms draped over the wheel, my breath fogging the glass. Marbles shifts in its blankets, chewing on the knitted tassels, finally pissing the bed. The sick, warm smell of urine fills the cab.

"Such a charming animal," says Reg, cranking down the window. Drops crater my upholstery. He pushes his face into the wind, then turns back to me. "Wouldn't it be a pity if doggy jumped?"

Reading my mind, I think. But I say, "Roll up my window or you'll be the one jumping."

"No wonder you were Mom's favorite," he says. "You're as uptight as the dog."

For weeks, the headlines in the *Fresno Bee* have been about the destroyed raisin crop. Picture after gory picture of flooded bunches, beards of mold. Harvests like mine, still on tray papers, waiting for the coming days of sunshine that won't matter. Waiting for the plow to turn them under. For once, I have a reason to be uptight. There have been many hot and dry summers, Augusts that fed the whole country. The fields used to ripple with pickers in liquid clouds of heat, as if they worked in a river, fifty men and women for every twenty acres. But since I've taken over the farm, the years have been wet and lean.

Ten minutes from home, the sun peeks through the clouds. A sign to make me hate God. A white shaft brightens the freeway ahead of us, turning puddles into sheets of chrome. The light spreads and I know somewhere there's a rainbow, but I refuse to look. We cross into the glare and I fish my sunglasses from the glove compartment. The Sierra Nevadas almost light up the eastern horizon, seeming to hold still out my side of the truck.

"Ain't it pretty, big brother?"

I shoot Reg a look that he should remember well from his little brother days, the fire that always crossed my eyes the moment before my fist crashed his mouth, gut, ears—whatever he left unguarded. Now my hands stay on the wheel, but I'm squeezing tight enough to leave fingerprints in the vinyl. Reg purses his lips, holds his breath. He looks at his wrist, no watch, and he tosses his hat onto the seat between us. My gaze finds his scalp.

"Pretty sad state, huh," he says, rubbing the stubble. "Finally had to butch it so I didn't wind up looking like—I don't know, the rings of Saturn, or something." He looks at my head. "It figures I'm the one losing my hair. You still have most of yours and you're not even using it. Speaking of, what's your poor wife feeding me tonight? I had nothing on the dick train except cardboard pizza."

"They won't be joining us."

He snaps a look at me that might have come from roadkill, huge eyes and wide, disbelieving mouth. "What is this? Uncle Reg comes home and everyone runs for the hills?"

"I need you to do something for me."

On cue, Marbles begins to pant, shrinking the cab around us. This time, it's me who rolls down the window.

Gradually he reads the task in my face and slides his stare to the dog. We've always been like this, Reg and me, with little need for words. A long breath winds out of him.

"I thought you just missed me." He puts on his hat and pulls the bill low, thumbs his bottom lip. "At least it's only a dog. I am kind of thankful that Mom didn't live too long. I might have a problem with that."

All around us, vineyards ripple like the surface of a rough, green sea. The soil has a slick, milk chocolate hue, the standing water too bright to look at. Turning onto my street, we can see the second story of my house over the foliage, windows catching the light in glossy squares. I remember building it, the thrill of seeing it rise from the dirt, all the hundreds of times Danielle and I scanned the horizon after being away—anniversary dinners, vacations to the coast—teaching Nicky to point and say *home*. Not once did I imagine it empty.

We've been home a few hours, but the contents of Reg's knapsack are scattered everywhere. Clothes drape the chairs and rumple on the floor. Cassette tapes spill onto the bed. He knocks a tin box off the nightstand edge and it clatters open, breath mints rolling out across the wood floor. Reg goes on unpacking as if deaf.

The hours I spent in this room, on hands and knees, putting Matchbox cars back into their bins, fishing crayons from under the bed, shelving Curious George and Dr. Seuss and twenty kinds of *The*

*B Book*, each time more angry than the last. But my son was never as messy as my brother.

"Did you guys move Nicky into the other room?" Reg asks. "Wasn't this Nicky's?"

My fists start to knot.

"None of his stuff's in here," he says. "Did you move him down the hall?"

"It's bigger," I lie. "You know, a growing boy."

Reg regards me cockeyedly. He presses his hands against his face, stretching the skin over round cheekbones, slanting his eyes. A boyish gesture, I think, except that a beard shadows him and coarse pores freckle his nose. There's nothing young left in his face. He says, "I'm calling it a day. Next time you talk me into a visit, you're springing for airfare."

"Fine," I say. "Good night."

I move through the house, turning off lights. I pause in the doorway of Danielle's old sewing room, the one I told Reg is filled with Nicky's toys—it's true, in a way. Boxes line the walls, stacked three high, filled with everything I couldn't look at another day. The boxes are worse than the clutter, a reminder my house isn't just empty, but drained.

When Danielle calls, I slide to the floor, cradling the phone to my ear. "Where are you?"

"Nowhere. Safe," she says. "We're not doing this again."

"I have a right to know."

"I'll hang up, Drew."

"Can I talk to Nicky?"

"It's not a good idea," she says. I hear her breathing, then a sigh. "Two minutes," she says, and puts him on the line.

"Buddy," I say. "Do you like where you're living now?" My son's quiet, still hurt, probably scared from what his mother's telling him. I try to speak lightly. "What's your school like? Who's your teacher? Tell me about her," I say. "Nicolas, answer your father," I say. "Sorry, buddy. Sorry." But apologizing sickens me and that makes me sound dangerous, which frightens Nicky more, and Danielle comes back on the line.

"He's crying again," she says. "What did you say to him?"

"Nothing. What'd you think, I cussed him out?"

"Screw you," I hear before I slam down the receiver. It's funny, I wait on nails for their call, and yet I'm the one who hangs up.

I scramble eggs with red peppers and lots of cheese, but Reg mashes them around with his fork. "Even Nicky eats better than that," I say. "Come on. I made them the way you like."

"No, you made them the way *you* like. If I eat any more cheese I'll shit a brick."

Marbles pushes its dog dish across the floor, a nails-on-chalkboard sound that makes us cringe. Reg stares at it, his face chiseled hard.

"Are you still working at that restaurant?" I say. "What's it called?"

"Black's," he says. "Still there."

I sock him in the arm. "My glamorous brother the dishwasher," I say. "How do you make a living? Really. You selling drugs?"

"That must be it. I obviously have a questionable moral stance, since my brother calls out of the blue and invites me home to kill a dog."

I meet his cold eyes head-on. I say, "And yet you're still here."

He turns back to Marbles. Only eleven months separate Reg and me. When Dad died, Reg wasn't speaking to any of the family but me, and even that was strained. Down for the funeral, he signed his part of the farm over without blinking. "Go ahead," he told me. "Be a farmer. Go buy a horse. Wear a belt buckle the size of a license plate, have three daughters named Sarah. But you better be good, because

Dad isn't here anymore to solve your problems." Even then I heard his warning, the world of relics I was tying myself to.

"Let me show you around the place," I say. "I planted new vines last October. Some things have changed, you know."

He stares at his hands, the soap-colored skin around his fingernails. "Show me," he says.

The dirt is muddy, scattered with puddles, but that's the only sign of rain. The skies are so blue they're almost white. The heat's come up, baking a dirty musk out of the ground. It's time to survey the damage to my crops, and I'm filled with the hope I'll find a little soggy fruit and nothing else—no blackening mold, no choking smells of rot—a harvest I can salvage. Out here, our memories boiling with games of Smear the Queer and flashlight black widow hunts, I'll tell Reg the truth about my family, explain that I need him to stay, maybe without saying much at all.

The ATV coughs to life and I pump the throttle, flip down the choke, swing my leg across the gas tank and step it into gear. Reg climbs on behind and locks his arms around my stomach.

I check our tracks as we go, hoping the tires are chewing deep enough to find dry soil under the wet topcoat, but I see only chocolate-brown. Not a good sign for a man hoping to find dry raisins. I cruise the dirt avenue that separates my acreage from my neighbor's. I miss the pheasant tail of dust usually being made this time of year, triangulating my place in the world. "Mr. Goodrich died the week after Mom," I shout. "Remember when you duct-taped his screen door shut?" But Reg can't hear me.

The paper trays hold water along with the harvest. I pop the Honda into neutral and step off to walk a row. The fruit remains partly grape, skin purpled by the sun, while inside there's a sugary juice not yet dried out. I kneel and lift a bunch. I can tell from the weight that it's been soaked. The berries sag like swollen glands. Lifting the corner of the tray, I find black mold. Down the row I find worse: fruit measled with fungus, sick ooze on the paper. I see my future in their dripping skins.

"Bad?" says Reg.

I drop to my ass, feel the mud soften underneath me like diapery muck. Every harvest, my dad wound himself as tight as a clock, muttering complaints about things he couldn't control, weather and liberals and wetbacks, and he had his busts, too—hell, Armageddons, episodes that had us crapping our jeans—but our family always healed. Our mom never snuck Reg and me away.

My brother lifts me by a fistful of shirt. I follow him, my caked pants moving like a cast. "Screw it," he says. "There's always crop insurance."

"Nope."

He can't hide the drop-off in his stare. "Next year then. Tighten the belt a little," he says, slapping my gut. He mounts the three-wheeler and revs the engine. "Get on," he says. "Come on. It's like a bicycle. You never forget."

I swing my leg behind him and Reg guns it. Mud slaps the fenders, roosters behind us. He climbs through the gears and the engine whines. My chin bores into the firm pack of Reg's shoulder and wind scratches my peeled eyes and I watch my harvest rush by, the details of ruin lost in speed. We go the length of the turn row, past the old pump and its wild chinaberry tree, cutting across to the old Goodrich vineyard. His uprooted vines lay scattered, ripped from the ground last fall. I feel Reg's stomach tighten at the sight of our old stomping grounds and he cranks to full throttle, turns hard. I lean in with him, but I know it's too sharp. We slide halfway into the turn before the wheel lifts and we get dumped.

We crawl from under the bike, laughing. No one would believe I've lost my harvest, my farm, my family. Laughing like an idiot with my brother, rolling up our jeans to check the burning places for deep cuts, I'm steadying.

We right the three-wheeler and I wear out my arm starting the engine.

"What's happened to this place?" he says.

"Just tightening the belt," I say.

I'd been keeping all the same habits since Danielle and Nicky left, as if I could bring them home by the force of routine. For the first time, I feel separate from Danielle and Nicky, all my pieces finally returned to me. I can work from here, I think, bring them home to live with a complete man, if only Reg will stay a while, short-circuit me enough so I can be rewired. I start by taking my muddy pants and tossing them in a wad on the kitchen floor. I can almost hear my mother's voice. Reg and me, coming to the door caked in mud, open sores scabbed with mud, mud gelling in our hair and caking in the grooves of our hands—Mom yelled, but Dad was the punisher. Afterward, she would enter our room with the softest voice and talk about all the complicated ways he loved us.

Four months ago, Nicky is saddled before me on the three-wheeler, his hands riding mine on the handlebars. He wears denim overalls and kid leather work boots. He balances our shovels across his lap, his with a cut handle and miniature head. He bobs under my chin, making soft concussions against my jaw. Summer heat has yet to descend and there's a cooling breeze and our flesh ticks with goose pimples. My vineyard's back forty acres are cursed with loose, sandy soil, and the Honda cuts a wake as it swims ahead. Weeks before, I'd set out ground squirrel bait—rodents had been digging craters around my vines and gnawing away the roots—and now a bucket of refill poison is strapped to the back of the Honda.

I brake at the homemade trap, an inverted *T* of black sewer pipe staked to the ground, the ends of the crossbar left open for the squirrels to feed. I lift the cap and look inside. They've eaten the thing empty.

"Dad," says Nicky, "shouldn't there be a bunch of dead squirrels lying around?"

"They usually die underground."

"It's possible, though, right?" he says. "What if I find a skeleton? Do you think it will stand up? Can I keep it on my windowsill?"

"Your mother would kill me. We're not bringing home skeletons," I say. "You'll be lucky if you find any bones at all."

The trap smells like whole grain. I examine the joints, the plastic crazed from solvent glue. I should have built it from white, thin-walled pipe, because I could have seen the level of the poison pellets as a dark mass inside, tracked the rate of descent. I see a patent in my future, a fortune—and Nicky walks up with a mound of poison cupped in his hands.

I slap his arms apart and the pellets fall, plant themselves in the dirt. "Dad," he says.

I kneel before him, brushing off the poison dust with my shirt. "Get on the three-wheeler," I tell him. "Now. Go." We tear away in a whirl of flying sand. I hold his hands together in my lap, praying he hasn't touched his mouth or rubbed his eyes, trying to recall if he has cut knuckles or open blisters. We reach the house and I carry him in, still cuffing his wrists together as if he'd committed a crime. I open the washbasin tap and hold his palms under the water, calling for Danielle.

"Keep his hands under the water," I say. "Don't even let him rub his own nose. I'm going to check the label."

The poison bucket flies the skull and crossbones. I read down the list of warnings, precautions, descriptions of what to do if swallowed. My eyes feel tight. How could he miss these signs? The goddamn skull—what does it say but death? How could I trust him to ever be alone? How could I send him to school, or go to work myself, when he doesn't know to leave poison alone? I feel my foundations going soft, my fists knotting as if they cling to ropes, the edges of my vision turning red. I storm back inside.

Nicky's face is buried in his mother's shoulder. She kneels, cradling his head. "You scared him to death," she says. "He thought he was dying."

"Did you wash with soap? Does he have any open cuts?"

"He's fine, Drew."

I grab Nicky by the hair and rip him from his mother. "Did you eat it?" I growl. He tries to hide his face but I clamp his chin. "Tell me if it got in your mouth, Nicolas. Tell me if you taste anything strange." Nicky goes wild trying to escape, arms and legs whipping, hands clawing at my face. I clamp down on him harder.

Danielle's trying to pull me back, her nails burning into my skin. And I push her away from me. Without looking. Hard. I feel the sting in my knuckles, the spent tension numbing my arm—she yells, I hear collapse. I turn. Danielle's curled on the floor.

Nicky goes to her, touches her shoulder, nuzzles her cheek. Both recoil from me when I reach to pet Danielle's hair. "Tell me you're okay," I croak. "I don't know—I'm sorry. I was just so scared, Danielle—"

Her hair coils over a cut on her chin, matting in the blood. She locks Nicky in the bathroom with her and I can hear the tap running and she won't open the door to take the bag of ice I bring.

I straddle the three-wheeler, peel into the vineyard. All around me, grapevines warp from the ground. Nothing's as grotesque as a grapevine, gnarled and hollowed, skin like ash. Even I'm better than grapevines. My heart begins to settle again into its cavity, my blood cools, the red circling my vision fades. I think of a hundred apologies, but I see at last that the love for my son is bottomless—the only problem? Nothing to be sorry for.

When I return home they're gone.

⚊⚊o

My hair's spiked from the towel, skin rasped clean. The conditioned air of my house chills me. "Reg," I call out. "I didn't even show you those new vines. You want to get some beers? Reg?" His room is empty except for the massive clutter. On the desk I find a half-written letter to someone named Elise, and it's a shock. Never did I think I could be tearing him away from his own life. I'd always imagined Reg alone, between women, and he hadn't mentioned anyone worth writing to. "Reg?" I shout down the hall.

I find him in the box room, standing in the center, hands dead at his sides. He doesn't turn when I step beside him. When he looks to me it isn't for answers. "You should have told me," he says.

"Who's Elise?"

He cocks his head. "How could that even matter to you?"

I shrug. He's right, but I'll do anything to erase the contempt in his eyes. I feel that slow closing of my hands.

"How long?" he says.

"Few months."

"How many months?"

I can't look at him. My vision is going scarlet. I feel this catapult tension in my arm, a springy restlessness, getting worse. I shift my weight from one foot to the other, crack my knuckles, pick at nothing on my lip. I have nowhere to hide this time bomb.

"Drew," he says. "Where are they?"

Breath throbs in and out of me. Fists hang like bricks, heavy and square.

"What in hell did you do?" he says, grabbing my wrist. I shake away but he holds on, the meaty part of his hand making a tight seal against my skin. "You gonna punch me? Is that what happened? What, Drew? Did you sock him in the nose for crying? Break his arm? What?"

I drop my fist on his arm and I'm released. Where he cuffed me the skin's raw and I guard it against my stomach. I wait for him to pounce, a single cougar leap, send us rolling down the stairs, like we did when we were kids, landing at the feet of our father, getting torn apart by his big hands. Reg doesn't move. "That's exactly what happened, isn't it?" he says, but I'm walking away.

I hear the bathroom lock click as I descend the stairs. I imagine him staring at himself in the mirror, his shaking hands and deliberate breath, the little inventories he'll take before he comes to talk with me.

I wait for him outside, acting like I'm fixing the busted three-point tractor lift, but the wrench is dead weight in my hand, falling off the corners of bolt heads and ringing against the concrete. I finally give up. When Reg emerges from the house, his knapsack hangs over his shoulder. Marbles bites at his heels, jumping for the ends of his fingers. With each step Reg takes, the dog works itself into more of a froth, its bark winding into a siren.

"Are you driving me to the station?" he says.

"I want you to stay. I need your help with a few things."

"I'm too old for fistfights, Drew. As for my other qualities—" Reg kneels to pick up the wrench, tests its heft. He looks at me, eyes narrowed, then full of sparks, awake. In a single fluid motion Reg wheels and brings the wrench head down, snapping Marbles spine between its shoulders.

He holds the wrench to me. "You're still just a kid, aren't you? I caught up and passed you. Isn't that something? I never thought that was possible. But—" He shakes his head, letting his thought trail.

When his voice returns, it's hard. "Next time, kill your own dogs."

My gaze lifts from the mangled body to my house rising behind us. There's a memory for every plank of siding and lately I'm thinking of them nonstop, all the sweet times drowning in a flood. But inside, nothing moves. "Stay, Reg. I can't be here alone."

Reg pulls the knapsack higher up his shoulder. He packed so quickly that his clothes overflow the top, pressing bulges into the canvas walls from the inside. His stare softens and slips away from me. He scans our landscape, the vines in rank and file, my house rising from the ground as if it were another thing planted in the dirt. If he goes, I know it's for good. I push past him and lift Marbles's limp carcass by the scruff. Its last act was to shit itself and the gruel-like stuff spikes the fur on its back legs. I carry it around the house, across the lawn to the chicken wire fence, throw it over. Reg gets a shovel for me and sits down cross-legged in the grass, watching, not a word between us. For this, at least, he'll wait. By nature we are impatient men.

# THE ATLAS SHOW

Atlas dressed for selling: wing tip shoes, slacks, dress shirt, his collar undone and tie loose around his neck. His short hair was combed back, still drying from the morning shower, and the cowl of skin connecting his jaw to shoulders glowed pink with a fresh coat of Aqua Velva. His body was squeezed in new clothes, already damaging the expensive reinforced seams. It wasn't enough to say he stretched everything out. His wardrobe constricted around him, popped buttons and exploded threads, because the man inside, my father, couldn't be contained.

"Coach going to bat you cleanup?" he asked me, spooning creatine supplement into half-glasses of water, stirring.

The drink Atlas pushed across the Formica to me was like white sand.

"Season starts next week," he said. "If he wants to win, better get his stars aligned."

I strained the mixture through my lips, watching Atlas gulp his own. He visited gyms, schools, the million-dollar homes of ex-athletes with nothing better to spend their fortunes on than the tension weights he sold, a dream job for an old lifter like him. I wondered if they saw themselves in Atlas, or what they were afraid of turning into. He'd been an alternate on the seventy-two Olympic team, missing glory, as he told it, "by one crummy ounce," and the chiseled muscle I'd seen in pictures had turned to heavy, dimpled flesh. It turned him into a clown, a jolly Santa Claus at Christmas, and he once put on a diaper as Baby New Year, the swaddling fastened with a huge novelty pin. Atlas was too happy to oblige. He believed he had a way with people, and I guess he did. But people laughed at his jokes, bought his barbells and weight benches and curl-up ramps, I thought, because they saw in Atlas what they didn't want to become. A big joke.

He patted down his pockets—chest, hips, butt—for his wallet and keys, but he stopped with his hand on the doorknob.

"Just how is practice?" he said.

"Fine," I said. "Warm."

"You're working on?"

"Fundamentals. Like always. But I guess that's college sports, huh?"

"Got that right," he said, going out the door. "It's just you've been quiet about it."

I pulled a hoodie sweatshirt over my head, all part of this show I put on. I was still living at home, acting out a plan that had blown up in my face: play for Clatsop Community College until I got a pro contract or a university scholarship. I'd once believed that the scouts and recruiters were lining up for miles. Now I brought in my bat bag every evening, let it sit by the door and lie for me, kept up this training regiment for nothing. I hadn't set foot on campus in three weeks. Atlas already had tickets to the first game, but I had no guts to tell him straight that I'd been kicked off the team.

"Bring Coach home for dinner," he said through the closing door. "Let Atlas work some magic for you."

He gave me the smile that, according to him, had sold ice to Eskimos.

His car was still fuming in the driveway when I stepped out. I waved, his features like a blob through the dewy windows. I hoofed it down the sloped bike lane, the squat taverns and offices so familiar I didn't see them anymore. The air broke good and crisp on my bare face while underneath my clothes I worked up a lather, a steadily bumping heart rate. Coming off the last plateau, the view of the river opened up.

Seeing the Columbia everyday was the only good thing about living at home. The water seemed a solid pane of glass, white in the sun, breaking into smaller pieces the closer I got. I turned onto the gravel streets skirting the bluffs, the big houses with broad, uncovered windows looking down on the marinas. Atlas had sworn to me all his life that when he made that perfect sale, he'd make one of these mansions ours. I'd been returning the boast since I first picked up a baseball bat, that I'd see him retired with his feet up in a La-Z-Boy, his view of the opposite shore picture perfect.

As usual, Columbia View Park was deserted and most of the boat stalls below empty, but I paused a minute, checked around me before jumping the low chicken wire fence and scrambling down the path I'd worn to the water's edge. I'd hidden the box of ragged baseballs, along with a bat and rubber tee, in a thrush of wild blackberries. I guesstimated the distance from my imaginary home plate to the opposite bank was about the same to the outfield wall of a major league park. I set up the tee, took out my bat, worked at controlling my breath. Ahead of me, the river seemed to be waiting in anticipation, barely licking at the rocks. The cigar raft of logs the mill was building rolled to and fro against the cradling stakes. Washington's hills weren't touched by mist, not a cloud overhead, and snowy Mount Saint Helens swelled into the blue.

I brought the bat to my shoulder. Fundamentals. Eyes on the ball, weight behind me, hips before hands. Muscle memory took over. Every coach I'd ever had said my body remembered everything. I started my swing easy, peppering liners back to where a pitcher would be, and watched them get swallowed by the river. I opened up and the ball arced high and splashed down halfway across. I wouldn't let myself hurry, rip a cold muscle. This was my future—all I had left of it, anyway. I aimed the next splashdown for the same place, kept my focus on reps.

I put another ball in the pike, my whole body singing. Hands high, elbow out. My swing cracked and I knew its distance before I was in my follow-through—the ball sailed over the water and came down on the other side, a home run ball to another state. The stuff of legend. I imagined myself trotting around the bases, the pitcher squatting there on the mound, destroyed.

But, of course, I stood there alone. This was not a path to glory. It wasn't even baseball. Except that if felt good, that humming in my hands, every muscle sure of itself, I didn't know why I bothered.

The night of Clatsop CC's first game, Atlas paced the hallways so hard I thought the carpet would ignite. It usually meant a big sale was on the horizon, tens of thousands of dollars on the line, one of those he bragged would change our futures, but tonight was about me. He leaned his massive shoulder to my room's door frame, measuring his breath like he was about to clean-and-jerk the world record.

"Don't you need be somewhere?"

I studied his face, his jaw tight enough teeth were ready to start popping. I pulled my workout hoodie on over my shirt.

"Someone from the college should have contacted you," I said, lacing my shoes. "That's weird. Weird no one contacted you."

"What's this about?"

"I ought to show you something," I said.

We had to park a block away from the river's edge and walk to Columbia View. A senior citizen band was bopping calmly in the gazebo, every inch of the grass covered with a blanket, a dancing child, someone's picnic dinner.

Atlas didn't say anything. He'd always been an optimist, my father, patient when it came to seeing the brightest in things, and in the car I'd felt him bucking up.

"Good idea, Junior. Getting me out of the house. I haven't been to one of these in years."

He flashed a smile, but it was crooked, a defect in his face.

Atlas ordered a dozen hotdogs from a vendor's stand and put the greasy box between us. He squeezed mustard and mayonnaise out of finger packs and downed them in three bites.

"Eat up," he said. "Don't let me make a pig of myself."

"I've got to watch my diet," I said.

The sound of him bingeing wrung my stomach like a rag.

We sat on the curb and listened to the music through the last song. Twilight was coming on and he looked blue in it, staring out at the stretch of water and the forested ridge beyond. I knew my chance but I couldn't explain what happened, why. He'd shown me pictures of the Greek Atlas all my life, the head pushed down under his burden of a planet—selflessness and perseverance, my father said, the most any man could manage. I'd lost both along the way.

People stepped around us but Atlas didn't move. He watched the musicians case their instruments as intently as he'd watched them play.

"What is it," he said at last. "A girl? Is coach hassling you?"

"I've had a lot on my mind," I said.

"Coach will find you a spot."

"No he won't," I said.

"Why won't he? What's that mean?"

I stared at the lights coming on around us, the houseboat windows in the marina, the scattered dots running up the hills on the other side of the water. I couldn't have shown him if I wanted. Not in the dark. Atlas wagged his head between his shoulders and I saw the top of his head, the scalp through greasy curls.

"Other men have had to pick themselves up," he said. "There's no shame in it, Junior."

He struggled to his feet and offered me his hand, looking down on me from that velvety sky. I think it was worse, him coming to his own conclusions, looking like he'd taken a cannonball to the gut.

"Don't look at me like that," I said. "It's not what you think."

"Atlas is just fine, but Little Atlas—we're still finding out how fine he is."

"I've got a tryout," I said, I didn't know why. "With the Mariners."

His hands dropped to his sides, jaw unhinged.

"A scout came to practice to see me. The guy couldn't wait for a game. Coach really hated it, said I was a distraction."

"So college?"

I ran my finger across my throat like a knife. "Who needs them?" I said.

His head started to bob, believing.

"There are no sure things," I said.

"Only sure people," he finished. "Good Christ, the big leagues. Why didn't you tell me?"

"Didn't want you to hang your head if I didn't get it."

Inside his thick body, he was trembling—I heard it in his voice, his breath.

"Not if another good thing ever happened to you. You're my son through and through."

He rocked back on his heels, hands in his pockets.

"What day?"

"What?"

"The tryout."

"Thursday."

"Where?"

"I've got the address," I said, getting to my feet.

"At the stadium?"

I didn't say anything but he rolled back farther on his heels.

"Think of that," he said. "A tryout in the stadium. They're not giving those things away, you know. That's a rare gem indeed. Will the manager be there? The big league staff?"

I shrugged.

"You know who else they did this for? Ken Griffey, Jr. Know who else? No one. Just a pair of juniors. I'll take the day off work, drive you up there."

"You don't have to," I said.

"A father has to."

"Atlas—"

He cupped my shoulder as if he handled something rare and rich.

"You know why I taught you to call me Atlas?"

"Everyone calls you that."

"But do you know why *you* do?" he said. "Because I didn't want you thinking there was a wall between us. If you don't know your dad, the human being, you don't know yourself."

He gave my cheek a gentle cuffing.

"You hear me?"

"Loud and clear," I said.

"But you're my son. I'm your old man. No denying it. That's what I'll be shouting from the top of the world. I'm the proud papa of the next Atlas."

Atlas polished his old wing tips and bought a wide silk tie that flashed like aluminum in certain angles, got his best suit dry-cleaned for the occasion. I must have caught some sleep before the big day, but I wasn't sure how. Maybe I was so much the fool's boy, I started looking forward to what wasn't coming.

We saw the stadium's light towers from I-5 rising among squat metal warehouses. We curled through the empty streets, following signs, and we heard freight cars shunting together with hollow bangs. Atlas circled around the stadium. Smash boards were across all the entrances and after coming back to where we started, he pulled to the curb. He looked at me cockeyed.

"They're expecting you?"

I pulled at a thread on my bat bag. I'd straddled it between my legs the whole drive, drummed on it nervously.

"We're going inside. Slide over behind the wheel."

He walked to the gate, shook it once or twice, then lifted it over his head in a smooth snatch. He wagged his head at me to drive the car through, then let the board down behind and got in the passenger seat, wiping his hands together.

"A little trespassing," he said. "Nothing major for the team's future star, right?"

Without any cars to break up the space, the lot stretched forever. I could have cut across the lines but switchbacked though the lanes.

"You dancing ballet all of a sudden? Drive right up. This is where you belong, isn't it?"

I stopped with the bumper a few feet from the main entrance. Atlas stepped out, looked around, lost.

"Well, superstar," he said to me, ducking his head down. "I guess we knock."

I might as well have been knocking to enter a stone for all the noise I made. Atlas motioned me aside, put his body close to the doors, pounded them with all his strength, fists and palms, shouting to open up, let us in.

"Maybe I had it wrong," I said.

He waited a moment, staring at me, then steeled his jaw, braced his knees, and threw his shoulder at the door. His face turned red and his knees looked about to buckle on the rebound, but he threw his body for me again, again until his lunging no longer shook the doors. He rested there with his shoulder flat on the metal, wilting.

"You've got to do your tryout," he said.

"I can't."

"Tell me why, Junior."

I curled my hands, cracked them open.

"It's impossible."

He nodded, dusted his palms together, opened the car. The engine was running before I had myself inside, the car cutting across stalls before I was settled. I thought we were blazing home, already worried about the silent hours ahead of us, but at the end of the lot he stopped. His breath rasped in and out and I thought I could feel the vibration of his heart shaking the car. Arms sagging off the wheel, sleeves hanging down as if they were empty, he turned down a road that ran along the lip of the Sound, passing the throats of industrial piers and numbered warehouses. Semi-trucks came up to our bumper, whipped by us the other direction. The road pulled away from the water and he nosed into a driveway, turned around, drove back the other direction. His stare wandered over the water and he forced it back to the street, only to slide again over the ripples.

"The Mariners' offices are downtown somewhere," he said.

"You been there?" I said.

"I called on them once. They didn't buy what I was selling, then, but we could try it."

I folded my hands in my lap.

"They wouldn't know who I was."

"You could let Atlas work some magic for you."

I just shook my head no and he went on driving up and down the same street, losing himself in water muddy and gray, nothing to say between us.

———

The room was on the fourth floor, crowded with two double beds and a dresser nailed to the floor, a table and chairs no one would want to steal. He had sworn he was too tired to make the drive home, but wouldn't give me the wheel, either. Atlas emptied his pockets, keys and change, slipped out of his shoes and jacket and slacks, unbuttoned his shirt cuffs and loosened his tie so it hung down his chest like a cut noose. He stretched out on the bed and clicked on the television but I knew from his face he wasn't really watching. We didn't even have a change of clothes.

"Are you hungry?" I said.

"I could eat."

I gathered the coins. I'd seen a vending machine down the hall and anything would do, anything to loosen this lockjaw silence.

"Take my jacket," he said. "It gets cold up here when the sun goes down."

I put it on. My arms felt like straw inside the sleeves, the shoulder seams coming down my arms so far I felt half my actual size. I fed the change into the machine, hoping nobody would walk past me in that bitch getup. Pre-packaged chili dogs with cheese and a bag of Corn Nuts filled my pockets before my money ran out. I warmed up the dogs in the microwave back in our room.

"Not exactly gourmet," I said.

"Food is food," he said.

"I ought to tell you, I didn't mean for us to wind up here."

His wide hand rose between us.

"Let me say this."

"I already know how it will sound."

"You don't know."

He raised his empty hot dog wrapper like he was toasting me.

"Other dreams will come along," he said. "Other chances."

"I'm glad you're happy."

"No one's laughing at you, Junior."

"I'm going to show you something," I said, pulling out my bat, stuffing baseballs into the coat pockets and then taking a handful more.

Atlas was on his feet.

"I'll go find us some drinks," he said, palms toward me. "Calm down and I'll go scrounge up something good."

I threw back the balcony curtain. Our reflections were all over the glass and with him standing far behind me we were almost the same size. I unlatched the slider and stepped out onto the little cage. The city lights burned below me except one dark hollow I judged to be the waters of the Sound.

"Watch," I said.

I threw a ball in the air but my swing was timid. I missed and the ball dropped to the ground.

"Come inside. You're going to hurt something."

The next ball was already in the air and my swing caught on the plastic patio furniture.

"Fucking crummy shit," I said, flipping the chairs over the railing.

"We're going to end up paying for that."

His voice sounded smaller, farther away from me than it had ever been.

I worked my feet up against the rail until the toes of my shoes were hanging over the edge. I tossed up a ball, rolled my hands onto the bat, pulled back my arms and let fly, the miracle swing. The ball shot into the night and I knew I had nailed it, that my father would finally see there was more to me than what he'd passed down.

But my back swing hit the slider door. Shatter, that was the exact sound it made, and the falling glass petered out like a rainstorm. Atlas was framed by it, staring at me, the wind moving the tails of his shirt. His legs in the boxer shorts looked bowed, stitched together with black hair, and his knees, swollen, like fat knuckles. The points of glass still hanging in the frame all pointed to him, to his wide, shallow face. His head began to wag back and forth at the glass stars on the ground between us.

"Back home I'd blast homers across the river," I said. "Into Washington."

His eyes lifted to where the ball had disappeared in the dark. Atlas stepped over the mess and stood with me on the balcony. His forearms flattened on the rail and he leaned out, squinting at the black.

"I believe you. That ball would have made the water. All the way to Japan."

Looking out with him, I thought I could almost see it going down with a fiery tail, entering the Sound with a hiss.

Atlas stepped into the room, took his pants from the back of the chair and pulled them on. He tucked in his shirt, tightened his tie. He wagged his thick fingers for the jacket I still wore and he buttoned it over his gut.

"I'm going to go confess," he said, "see about the damage."

He opened the door a crack and stopped without looking back at me.

"What's next for you?"

I shivered in the cold wind, dead quiet.

"I might talk to my boss," he said. "There's always room for good guys willing to learn."

He glanced at me sideways, once, and that was that. I didn't so much as shrug. He passed through the door with his back to me and it latched shut behind.

>———o

I would sell my textbooks for fractions of what I paid to help with the cost of the glass and then find I couldn't stop purging, would get rid of my bats and gloves and baseballs. I rode to work with Atlas until I'd saved up enough for an apartment, then we'd get coffee, trade customer stories, share the same buddies, and I got to know how other people saw him. Once I started to tell a couple of the guys about my time in the river league and Atlas blasted into the office with a big sale electrifying his smile.

He stopped in the threshold, locked his legs, took hold of the lintel and pushed—his knees buckled and strain glowed in his scarlet cheeks and gritted teeth, his arms bulging and trembling. His eyes popped open, feigning loss of strength, as if he'd topple and drop us all, and I grabbed my seat in a rush of imbalanced fear. But Atlas struggled back to the balls of his feet, flexed his hands on the header, and jerked his body straight. He held that pose, that hero's grin, letting us believe we'd all been saved. They gathered around him, slapping his back and shaking hands, congratulating him, for what they had no idea—for another Atlas Show, for making us laugh.

For the first time, I'm glad for this good life he's given me. Without him, I'd still be making myself a fool, flicking at the water with a stick. Now I stand on my own feet. When he comes to me, his face red with exertion, swollen, I shake his enormous hand. "Good one," I tell him. "Thought we were goners."

# CANDELARIO

andelario came back to our vineyard to work a fifth harvest in a row. I remembered his mangled body, the left elbow pointing into his ribs and the dwarfed hand dangling palm-out, the only two fingers like twisted fangs. "Know how he got that way?" our father said, lifting Candelario's arm, then letting go, letting it bungee at his side. "It's from all those years of outworking everyone with one arm tied behind his back."

Candelario lifted his chin and howled, laughing. White whiskers dotted his sharp Adam's apple. Gray curls billowed from under his hat.

"I bet you, okay," said Candelario, pointing at me and my brother. "You two, put together, I still pick more trays, bet?"

We both shook his good hand, the left one. The palm was one impenetrable callus; rice-like scars flecked his brown, almost black skin, the back ridged with veins. We bet two days' worth of trays.

"You boys," our father said, wagging his head. "You boys will not know what happened."

———o

All year we'd been preparing for the raisin harvest, our family's only crop, building momentum from winter pruning through the long irrigation season. Then, the week before, the middles were carved into terraces, the dirt between rows angled to catch the sunshine and shed water in the event of rain—a dirty word in August. Everything was shifting into a higher gear, speeding up. The night before picking started my brother and I were put to work sharpening the grape knives.

Our father kept the knives in an old sweatbox. The spiders had had a year to weave nets inside. He dumped the box on the workbench and black widows ran from the pile, most of which he smashed with the pad of his callused thumb. Their webs, as thick as fishing line, stuck to the knives. The blades were curved, a wing of flat steel from wooden handles, loops of twine for the wrist, all black from use. Our father gave us each small whetting rods and a can of 3-in-One Oil to share.

"I don't see why they can't do it themselves," my brother said.

I understood why. The pickers were always laughing, drunk, or sleeping. Our father had to kick their boots to rouse them from the shade. They only pretended to listen to him. We would be the butt of their jokes, in Spanish, the farmer's sons picking grapes, stealing wages. This crop looked like our best yet, green bunches swollen tight, a score of them on every vine, but the Mexicans wouldn't care. They'd keep laughing and boozing, lazy wetbacks. I'd picked last year. This was my brother's first time.

I liked being the authority every time our father turned his back. I'd stop my brother every couple strokes. "Look," I'd tell him, "you can't fidget so much, it'll round over the blade, you've got to make long clean strokes, like this." I showed him how, pushing the inner curve down the greasy block until the cutting edge gleamed. Watching him, I thought my brother was a hyperactive putz. He wasn't good enough. "You're not ready for this," I said. "You're a hyperactive putz."

But I made sure he found a good knife for himself, one without nicks or twists in the blade, with a smooth, comfortable handle—almost as good as the one I chose for myself. Then, after the rest of them were put back in the sweatbox, and the box put on the vineyard trailer, and the trailer hooked to the Massey Ferguson tractor, we worked extra to make our knives the best.

Candelario's arrival marked the start of our harvest.

That morning the trailer deck was loaded with bundles of paper trays; in a cardboard box were the payroll cards, a stapler, a fat black marker; there were wrenches and screwdrivers, just in case, and a five-gallon bucket of gloves, and the sweatbox of knives, of course. An iron tank filled with drinking water was roped to the bulkhead and wound in a musty canvas sheet to try and keep it cool; the spigot was bandaged with rags, black, gangrenous, and a tin cup leashed by a yard of new twine knelled against the metal. It wasn't water for me or my brother—our father would bring out two thermoses clicking with ice cubes.

Riding out, our legs dangled off the trailer. The unmatched tires knocked dust from the turnrow. Candelario's good hand jumped from the tractor's steering wheel to the throttle. The bad arm coiled in his lap like thick rope. A red handkerchief, fastened to his dirty cap, fell down the back of his neck and hung on his shoulders like a woman's hair. It looked ridiculous. "He's got a fag's hat," I told my brother. I was already spending Candelario's pay—our winnings—on a Schwinn ten-speed.

He stopped the tractor and trailer where our family's vineyard met the board and wire fence of a turkey ranch. We could see the birds moving between the gaps, white feathers and pink heads, hear their gobbling, smell their juicy stink.

Candelario tripped stepping down from the tractor. The empty butt sack of his jeans hit the ground and for a moment he was obscured inside a dust cloud, then I saw him gathering up the hose of his ruined arm like something spilled. Another picker helped him up. A little ring of Mexicans gathered around and slapped him on the back, saying things in Spanish.

I could taste the wind in my teeth as I shifted into tenth gear, speeding down the long asphalt driveway away from the house, and the vineyards bordering both sides became nothing more than a green blur.

My brother and I picked a row together. Keeping to the low part of the terrace, with knees pushed into the berm, I showed him what to do. Touch the knife to the stem, cup the bunch with your empty hand, then flick your wrist. Just a flick of the wrist—let the blade do the cutting. Just guide the bunch into the pan, soften its landing. When the pan's full, build a bottom row on the tray paper behind you, then spread up from that. Give the fruit room to dry in the sun. "You got it," I told him, settling down to work.

"Thanks," he said.

"It's only picking grapes," I said, trying on one of our father's phrases.

Candelario worked a row over from us. The right leg dragged a little behind him. That whole side of his body, it seemed, was riddled with bad luck. After he cut with the grape knife, his bunches dropped straight into the pan, and when he turned to spread he locked the pan between his hip and elbow, his good hand flat underneath. The bunches tumbled out, shattering on the trays, loose berries rolling into the dirt.

"Okay?" he said, popping his head under the vines, looking down our row. "You must go much faster." Within an hour he was a ways ahead of us.

I told my brother to ignore his example, to keep working the right way. He pulled farther ahead, doing two vines to one of ours, his one hand beating our four. It was a monster of a crop. The bunches grew so tightly together under the vines that getting the knife hooked on the stem wasn't easy. The trays were heavy with fruit and the high part of the terrace was crowded with trays.

"He's losing half the fruit," I said, snapping the knife, cupping the fruit into the pan.

"He's been doing it for a long time, I guess."

"For other people," I said. "This is our crop. He doesn't care, he's the same as any of them, but we have to care. That's our real job here, to care."

Then Candelario started singing. The melody was rough, his voice more timbre than note, the words in Spanish. It echoed in the distance he'd put on us, rubbing our faces in it.

So I started moving my mouth like I was a singing monkey, one arm behind my back, slashing at the stems and then shuffle-dancing like a Mexican up to the trays, then to the next vine. I dragged my foot, plowing a crooked line in the dirt behind me. My knife hand cut the air, conducting an invisible mariachi. My brother laughed and laughed.

A minute later I noticed the singing had stopped. My brother had stopped laughing. Down the row, Candelario was watching me. "You like music, *changos*?" He sang: "Well since my vaby left me all I found a new place to dwell nah nah all it's down at the end of lonely street in heartbreak hotel all well ah I feel oh so lonely vaby I feel oh so lonely vaby I feel ohso lonely I could die."

Later he shouted at us through the vines: "Faster, *pendejos*, I'm slowing down to not humiliate you. Okay?"

Near quitting time he popped his head through the canes and watched while we worked toward him, doing nothing but watching. "Want to know what happened?" he said when we got close enough to hear him hiss. "I got sucked between a tractor tire and the fender. Snapped the bones into tiny pieces until my arm wrapped all the way around the wheel. They took me to the hospital instead of paying me my wage. Said paying for a hospital bed was being generous."

We kept our hands moving, slice and guide, slice and guide, next bunch, next bunch, again and again. The middle of the row was dense with fruit and the trays lay edge to edge to hold the crop. Bunches thick around as forearms. Berries as big as our thumbs.

"Do you hear me?" said Candelario. "I didn't get my money! I was around your age, working for a guy just like your papa. He acted like him. Looked like him. I cursed them, sorry *gringos*. I cursed them and their farm."

His face was framed in the cascade of green leaves. "Fucking *changos*," he said.

Then he went back to work, breaking out in song, a harsh voice, a hoarse scratch, the words we didn't know.

"You think that's true?" my brother whispered.

"He's crazy," I said. "Just a busted-up old man."

My blade sliced at the stems and bunches dropped to the pan untouched, like they did for Candelario. My brother followed suit. Together we achieved a manic pace. Still his singing got farther and farther away, verse by verse, vine by vine by vine.

We tried all week to catch up—tried and failed just to keep from falling farther behind—but he worked effortlessly ahead of us. With the harvest half complete, he was scores of trays up, maybe hundreds. More. Worse, he'd tattled on us to our father. "You boys are there to work," he'd scolded that night at the supper table. "If you're not old enough to behave, you're not old enough to get paid. Period. Making fun of the poor old guy. Why don't you show some respect for your elders? And your boss, I might add. He's your boss, least when I'm not around."

By that time, the other pickers had become a rattling noise around me. My joints moved easily with the motion of picking, but everything else hurt. Nights I lay in bed and my body felt tight and brittle. Even the wrinkles in the sheets pressed into my back like steel wires.

"We're getting killed by a one-armed man," my brother said.

"Pointing out the obvious," I said.

We'd spent hours whispering in our dark room only to draw this conclusion. We were hopelessly swindled. Feeling wrung out in the hot sheets, thirsty, I shifted in the top bunk. In this exhaustion, this encompassing rage, breathing hurt my windpipe.

I said, "It's gotten bigger than a bet—family pride's at stake, the farm itself. He's having fun with us. He thinks we're a joke. I hate his guts."

"What're you gonna do?" my brother said, rhetorically, yawning.

I took a sore breath before I explained what.

Next we were downstairs in our father's office. We'd succeeded in descending the steps without waking up our parents. We only turned on the desk lamp, a dim hole of light in the dark room. Unrolling the grocery sack of white payroll cards, unrolling slowly, slowly to keep the paper quiet. The cards inside were gritty from the vineyard. Smudged by dirty thumbs. The tray count was circled in one corner, one card per row, and bundled by picker. We found Candelario's stack.

His writing was chopped, all corners and jagged lines. The letters *a* and *e* were mirror images of correct. "He's not really left-handed," I whispered, feeling a little sorry for him, even as I took them. We crept back up the stairs with his cards—his entire earnings—bowed in my hot palm.

We had him now, the great Candelario, the singer, the fastest man in the field—he was losing to a couple kids. Strictly by the books, in fact, he hadn't picked a single tray. We hid the cards in my dresser drawer. We'd saved our good name.

The last forty acres had the feel of a new race. To us at least. Candelario made a point of working a row over and putting distance between us, showing off. "*Changos,*" he crooned through the vines. "Monkey-boys. I'm breaking you. I'm breaking you."

We worked deliberately, easily, knowingly. We didn't give him the satisfaction of trying to keep up anymore.

Last day, payday, lunchtime, the pickers burned the blue tray wrappings and cooked their little logs of tinfoil next to the fire. The smoke, braided with blue ink, curled into the high sky. One by one they barehanded the food from the fire's edge, juggling and flapping and laughing until they could peel back the silver and eat. The smell of chili peppers, beans, butter, tortillas. My brother and I watched from a distance. "And he calls us monkeys," I said. "I bet they'll be farting nonstop."

Candelario approached, a pair of burritos in hand, the foil peeled halfway back. "There are extra. You want these?" He held them out. "We should be *amigos*. You finished the whole fields."

"They're our fields," I said. "Of course we finished."

But my brother—no sense of the moment—took the food. Candelario turned his back, his arm wagging as he shuffled away. My brother pinched a little from the tortilla and blew a stream of air at the hole he made. The stuff inside, whatever it was, threw a coil of steam back at him. "It's hot," he said. "It doesn't look bad."

I looked at the burrito my brother held out to me. "I'm not going to eat that."

My brother took a bite, chewed with his mouth open. I smelled the breath. After a minute he put the other burrito in the dirt between his feet and went on eating. I waited for his head to be engulfed in flames. For his belly to burst, his teeth to melt. I'd heard a few stories about their food. My brother stayed in one piece, however—breathing hard and sharp, a little watery around the eyes, a little red of the face—shame, I thought. Spontaneous combustion would have served him right.

Then our father was finally coming with the payroll. His truck was down the turnrow, crawling at us slowly so the dust wouldn't kick up.

He handed the checks to Candelario; Candelario passed them out to the pickers, gimping from one to another. Our father came toward us. "You boys have been working hard," he said, but that's all the payment he had for us right then.

Beyond him, Candelario passed out the last of the checks, and he looked at the one left in his hand. He'd only been paid for a few days, a few hundred trays. He turned our direction, staring holes in our father's back. I saw his mouth move but didn't hear the words. The whole crew of pickers looked at us then, getting quiet. Our father heard all their silence and looked back. Candelario approached unevenly, as if the left side were trying to shed the right.

I said, "Candelario sings while he works."

"You told me," said our father. "And I told you it doesn't matter."

"He shatters the bunches, too. I saw him do it a thousand times." I stepped between them, facing Candelario. I pulled the edge of his payroll cards out of my hip pocket just enough that he could see. His face changed. I said, "He's rough with the fruit. Look at his rows and you'll see berries rolling all over the place. Probably because he's got only one arm."

"Jesus Christ," said my father, putting his hands on my shoulders. "Forgive him, I don't know why he's acting this way."

"His singing makes up for it, though. It's not bad, his singing. Let my dad hear you sing."

The lines on the old man's face deepened, lips pinched, closer to spitting at my feet than breaking out in song. Behind him the embers withered in the cooking fire, and the shifting wind smelled of smoke, and a spark shot up, bright in the air.

"I bet you dance, too," I said. "How do you say 'dance'?"

"Dance," said Candelario.

"In Spanish, *por favor.*"

"*Bailar,*" he said.

"Do some *bailar* for us, too."

My father shook me, pulling me around, and he saw my fingers still on the cards, figured it out, and the game was over, I was going to die. My father was going to kill me. "What have you done?" he asked me. "What in hell have you done?"

Then I heard Candelario's feet begin to shuffle, raising puffs of dust. His boot heels drummed on the hard dirt, and the soles began to snap up into the air. He dropped the cap with its skirt on the ground and danced circles around it. Head bowed and good arm folded behind his back, the other swinging at his side, the palm twisting with his steps, a partner. He pranced figure eights around the fire, the hat. We could almost hear the guitars strumming, watching him dance. *Bailar.* The incantation stopped everyone in time.

When Candelario stooped to pick up his hat, dusting it against his thigh, the trance broke.

Our father talked to Candelario, standing apart, just the two of them. I thought back to him lifting the bad arm, letting it fall—he didn't touch him now, but gestured in the air around him. Candelario's face remained down, his bad arm shrunken at his side. The other pickers murmured, watching from the corners of their black eyes, saying what I could only guess.

Our father herded us to the truck. I sat between him and my brother, even though I was older—my feet on the hump, knees almost to my chin, feeling the drive shaft's vibration drilling in my heels. "The crop's down," our father said. "That's what matters. We're done with them now. They're done with us."

I remembered looking back through the cloud of dust. One of

them was kicking dirt on the last of the fire. Another took a drink from the water tank. There was a group already walking away, small swaggering figures in the rippled heat.

"What about us?" my brother said. "We worked just as hard as anybody."

"You boys pulled a stunt," our father said, wagging his head, wagging his head and starting to laugh. "There will be consequences. Don't think you've got away with anything. I promise you there will be consequences," he said, still laughing and laughing.

It let us breathe, that laughter. We didn't believe the consequences would be so bad.

That night clouds rolled in, thick, gray, signaling rain. The next morning's light spread slow and dim under the lid and the air could have been measured in pounds. Our father walked with his face to the skies, watching and waiting, calculating. If the wind started whipping the vines, he'd know the crop would get wet. We knew this. Everyone who grew raisins knew this. Rain could turn a perfect crop into a field of worthless, molding fruit. The packers wouldn't buy it. A starving coyote wouldn't even nibble. We'd have to plow it all under—the corners of the paper trays would stick out from the overturned dirt like little flags, blanching white in the sun. We'd have to live a year on meager crop insurance and hope to have better luck.

I'd been through that before, once, the year before Candelario first came to us. It poured on the crop and we almost lost our vineyard. What I didn't know—still to this day don't know—is if Candelario moved the world to protect or attack us? The crop stayed dry that year he danced the fields and he hasn't returned since. Years later I took over the vineyard from my father and have two boys of my own. I wonder, sometimes, if by some miracle he'll come back to pick my harvest. But why would he? He's always known there are no repairable men.

# BROTHER RHINO

I knocked over the barbecue and ruined it, the party, and the summer. The propane tank rolled off its cradle and lay on its side, like the exposed belly of a rare rhino, hissing an ominous death note. Burger patties and hot dogs and the blackened grill lay scattered, smoking from the lawn. My father's employees gathered around to look at what I'd done, and Father screwed down the propane valve so we didn't all explode. He looked at me and didn't say anything, as if there were no words to sum up my mistake.

"If we were a briquettes family," my mother said, kneeling with a plastic sack to pick up the meat before the dog did, "you'd have burned down the house."

She was trying to speak jovially.

"I was playing blind man's bluff," I explained.

"By yourself?" Father said. "Who plays that by themselves?"

Our backyard was crowded with a few grandparent types, many more aunt and uncle types who brought their children, little cousin types who looked up at me from the lip of our pool, waiting for an explanation. I'd been bumping into people. Twice I'd almost stepped off into the water. I didn't understand it myself, why no one was joining in.

Father was wagging his gray head. Hands hipped, feet apart, his legs scissors. Once upon a time my big brother and I would try to race between his legs before they closed, trapping us. Now I thought that if I tried, and he trapped me, he'd want to slice me in two.

"I don't know what we'll do for food," he said. His employees were looking to him for answers. He took questions seriously. He gritted his teeth and tried not to cry.

"I'll whip something up," said Mother, going inside with the heavy bag of ruined lunch. "Sandwiches, or I'll call for pizza. Crisis averted," she told my father.

She closed the door behind her, the sunlight silver on the glass. The old dog came over and sniffed her trail before dropping himself on the concrete stoop. I had to step over him to get inside. He'd been mostly my brother's dog. He missed my brother more than he would have missed me, I think. I bet my father and his employees sighed with relief when I left.

My mother stood before the sink, tap running. The garbage was slumped like a dead thing on the linoleum. She didn't turn around to see who had followed her in, she just kept holding onto the edge of the counter with both hands. I passed through the kitchen. I stopped in my father's den.

The gun cabinet was empty now. The light inside was off. It used to hold a hunting rifle, spotlighted. He'd take it out and polish the stock, disassemble and clean the chamber even though he hadn't fired it since the last cleaning, explaining muzzle velocity to my brother and me, kick, other terms we didn't understand but loved. I used to dream of hunting the rare white rhino with it. My father didn't think it could bring down something so huge as a rhinoceros, not of any color. I wasn't so sure I trusted him anymore. I knew one shot from that rifle could knock me backwards into the wall. One bullet could tear through skin and bone, releasing a hiss of blood. My brother had proved him wrong.

My mother turned on the light. She crossed the room to me, drying her hands on an apron she'd just put on. "Why do you always want to come in here? Like you just can't help it."

"Sorry I messed up."

"Only a barbecue," she said, kneeling to my level. "It didn't hurt you any? You're not burned?"

I told her I was fine, but she was already pushing my face into the dense, sun-smelling darkness of her hair. In there I could forget about all the accidents I'd caused. I could pretend my father would plan another barbecue before summer was out. I could close my eyes and see my brother—he rode past on the back of a white rhino, looking down at me. The rhino's steps shook the ground. A distance away he stopped and turned. He started to charge.

# RETREAT

People see my sun-cracked neck and arms, also the pale skin sliding out of my sleeves, and think *day laborer, truck driver, field worker.* True, I'm not the tweed and beard prototype of my chosen profession, but people have me pegged all wrong, and I don't mind telling them so. My classes meet in vineyards and orchards more than in air-conditioned rooms—hence the farmer's tan. My office is in the corner of a corrugated metal shed, a sign over the door reading *Dr. Wayne Heinrichs, Agricultural Science: He Grows On You.*

I'm known as a good guy around the university, despite my looks.

Of course, we are not on campus, but on faculty retreat, here in a coastal paradise. And my wife, Eve, instead of showing a little gratitude for coming along and getting into the spirit of these things, she's treating me like jailor or devil—got me which is which. Her hair hangs in long wet ropes down the back of the hotel robe. She's filing her nails, and bottles of polish are out on the vanity, and now and again she bounces icy stares off the mirror.

"You remember the drill," I say. "Johnson will hand us a party schedule. *9:07, dancing; 9:31, cease dancing, drink cocktails.* That man's rectum and head are growing closer together. He wrote a thirty-point agenda for tomorrow's meeting. Did I tell you? Be glad, honey, be thankful you've got a day free."

"By myself," says Eve.

She lifts her suitcase onto the bed and unzips the lid, but stares, movement suspended, so perplexed by the clothes folded inside.

"Remember how last year Johnson and his wife wore matching outfits?" I say. "They tried to play it off like it was a coincidence, all cute, remember? I was thinking, wouldn't it be a riot if we dressed alike?"

"Wayne."

"I took some liberties," I tell her, lifting a shirt identical to my own from her suitcase. I drop a pair of tan slacks around her size on the bed. I say, "Did you know you don't own any white socks?"

"You went through my things," she said, crumpling down on the quilted bedspread.

"We're playing a joke here. All you've got to do is walk through the door wearing these and the roof will come down."

"All so you can laugh at Jackson?"

"Johnson. I've worked with him for ten years. You've been coming to his shindigs all this time."

"I know his name," she says, leaning to the mirror, strumming with one finger the wrinkles crowding her eyes. I put the slacks back into the suitcase and spread the shirt on top. She says, "That will make you happy, that little getup?"

"I'm not going to force you to do anything. Judas F. Priest."

"Last time I'll do this," she says. "Promise me."

I raise my hands, promise, say, "Stick a needle in my eye."

Next day I watched out the window at people strolling the boardwalk along the bluffs, listening to the calls of seagulls and the sound of breakers eating the sand, and where was I? In faculty meetings, bludgeoned with Roberts's Rules of Order. Retreating. Eve does not appreciate the fact that afterwards I'm ready for some yucks, that I must stretch my legs or die. Her long, tan coat is wrapped around her clothes and the wind presses the edge against her legs as we walk. The breakers start way out, and the ocean looks platinum against the horizon. So it's not the prettiest day. The boards give a little underfoot and the air's fresh and I admit, I wouldn't mind being out here alone.

We pass a little gravel lot where a few cars are parked. The ground slopes away to a boat launch, and I hear things happening but we're running late already. Next thing I'm walking by myself. I turn and see Eve frozen in her steps, watching. A gang is dragging a pair of motor-boats—rafts, Eve calls them—into the water, the words *Surf and Rescue* emblazoned on the sides. Black wetsuits. Yellow helmets crowning their heads. They sprint the boats into the waves and lower the screws and become white lines toward the horizon.

On the beach, two kids squat around tide pools. Their parents balance-beam on the slick rocks, stepping over the white pools and broken surf. In the lot, there's a surfboard jutting out the back of a Subaru; a man is asleep behind the wheel. Pedestrians are moving up and down the boardwalk and cars continue rattling the short bridge over the inlet. No one seems aware that rescuers have taken to the water, that there are only a handful of reasons for doing so.

Eve and I, we're too aware.

Our Joey was four years old when he slipped out of the yard, in our little town of Caruthers, where things aren't supposed to happen. Eve grew hoarse from calling his name. Her legs, rubber from walking the neighborhood, high-stepped at last through the plowed field behind our house, following tracks punched in the soft dirt. She found him in the irrigation canal, near the end of his tracks, wedged against a flow gate with a nest of sticks and foam gathered around him. She pulled him from the sour water, but didn't hold him and cry into the sag of his neck—she stretched him on the dirt and then couldn't touch him again, that heavy sponge wearing our son's dinosaur shirt, his shoes with flashing red lights. She didn't call an ambulance or the police or a fireman or even pray. She called me at the college and told me to come home, that she needed me. I drove forty-five minutes not knowing a thing. Then she led me to the body. I had to scare away crows, and Eve? She stood behind and watched. She followed as I carried Joey to the house. All she could have seen was our boy's slack feet and lolling, heavy head, and she was barely even weeping. Since then, I don't know what she sees.

Now Eve retrieves a pair of sunglasses from her purse. There's no ring of thrashing water or boat sinking behind the horizon, but she won't look away. Her toes are at the lip of the sandstone bluffs and her coat wrinkles like a sack. I tug at her sleeve.

"Don't paw me."

"We're already late."

"Go on without me," she says—but how can I do that?

She doesn't move until two white lines are drawing fast toward shore, and then she's hurrying down the ramp. I follow her past the truck and the trailer parked on the launch, my smooth-soled loafers sliding across the treads in the cement. I can already read *Surf and Rescue* on the wet hulls coming our way.

The first one beaches and the rescuers dismount and pull the boat up the shore by crisp routine, in perfect reverse of departure. Two men carry a black bag up the landing ramp and toss it into the truck bed. The second raft lands on the beach. One of the men has a surfboard under his arm, a strand of kelp saddling the edge. He trots up the ramp, lays it in the truck bed, wipes a slick of water from his wetsuit and climbs behind the wheel. The others remove their helmets, hair spiky and wet. No banter between them, no laughter or grins.

The rescuers pass us with turned-down faces, except for one man whose eye Eve manages to catch. His hair grays around the temples and I could smell the ocean on him. He puts a hand on her elbow.

"Everything is okay. Just a little trouble. You go on, you have a good time. Let us worry about it." He lifts himself onto the tailgate and offers me a reassuring smile as the truck pulls away.

Eve turns back to the waterline. "Wayne, look," she says.

One of their yellow helmets, imbedded in the sand like a shell. She picks it up and wipes the grit with her palm, wet and coarse and clinging.

"Probably should leave it there," I say.

"Why would they be so careless?"

"You should leave it where they left it. They'll realize it's gone and be back."

But she hurries to the roadside, calling out and holding the helmet aloft in the air to the rescuers already out of sight.

"Did you see how exacting they were? They were machines." She holds the helmet to me like proof. "Whatever they found rattled them."

She wants me to take it, inspect it, offer a real opinion.

I say, "Mistakes, Eve. That's all. They happen."

She looks at the helmet like an impossible thing, a souvenir brought back from a dream. She arranges the chinstrap so it curves along the top of the yellow shell and holds it before her, as if she means to put it on, as if one could know the unknowable wearing it.

At the party, I pull aside one professor with a sense of humor, name of Davidson, the sleeve of his jacket kiting between my fingers. He's looking at me sideways, thinking—what? That he's thinking is enough. The whole point of a retreat is to get us all to stop thinking our usual things. To *retreat* from our thoughts. He shakes Eve's hand. The bangles she wouldn't leave behind slide on her wrist, swatches of bright color in the otherwise khaki room. "How are you?" he says, odd smile.

"I don't know. My feet hurt."

"Honey, show him," I say. "Give us a turn, show him the outfit." Eve opens her arms and the cloth spreads like fins. "What did I tell you? Aren't we twins?" I repeat her motion but with flourish, spreading my wings like I could fly to the ceiling. I say, "Remember Johnson last year?"

"What's with the helmet?" says Davidson, which Eve carries pressed against her hip, a holster.

I thought they'd be rolling, seeing us. A pair of my old work boots are lashed to her ankles and her hair's pinned in back, parted along top like mine. The shirttails nearly touch her knees and the short sleeves hang wide, past her elbows. She would need three, four of her to fill it.

Davidson is a lost cause. I start toward another group by the ocean view window, but Eve catches my arm. "Why don't you stand here and talk to *me*," she says. "You've been pointing me out to all these people but haven't introduced me to a soul."

"You *know* all these people. For chrissakes, ten years, Eve. Christmas parties, gift exchanges, the goddamn honors night. You've been friends with these people."

Eve scans the room, not really looking, just glazing by faces, then she's through the glass doors at a trot, out onto the balcony. I follow, resting my arms on the iron railing. There's no moon in the sky, the stars are behind clouds, and a cool wind whistles across the slowly closing door. Below there's a restaurant terrace. People eating, I guess, like people do on the terrace of a restaurant. A few couples brave the cold at ironwork tables. One woman is breastfeeding, a blanket covering all but the baby's buggish bare toes. A waiter moves between tables, white apron, black tie, pencil tucked behind his ear. Beyond, waves are rushing the shore, cracking over rocks, hissing back into the night.

"That's him," says Eve, whispering sharp in my ear. She's got a grip on my wrist. With the other hand she points. "The man from the rafts. He was the one I spoke to."

The woman with him wears an orange dress that almost matches her hair; he's in a black turtleneck with gray slacks. His face turns up, looking for stars, smiling.

"No more of this tonight," I say.

"Why shouldn't I wonder, Wayne?"

"So they dragged up a surfboard. So what?"

"So there's a mother suffering somewhere."

I feel the corner of my mouth, my lips opening, and my voice booms, coarse as gravel, not really like mine at all. In fact none of this is like me, the colleague that people on the other side of the glass know, or the husband my wife knows, or the good-natured guy I believe myself to be. "To you!" this other voice calls down to the terrace. "My wife saw you this morning. She thinks you boys in the rescue squad are doing a bang-up job."

Faces on the terrace lift. Stares touch and pass. The rescuer offers a guarded smile, nods, then turns back to the menu. The woman plays with her ear, her hand underneath her long, red hair.

The voice says, "She thinks you're tops, except that you left this behind." I grab the helmet from her hands. I lift it so he can see what he's done.

"That's enough," says Eve. The party behind us is becoming silent, too, this voice crashing through the windows.

"She's been going on about this helmet. She wasn't sure what you brought back to shore today so she talks about a goddamn helmet. So what's the scoop? Let us in on the secret so we can get some sleep tonight."

"Please," she says, trying to pull me around by the shirtsleeve. The rescuer holds my stare, arms folded across his chest, all tough guy but a bemused smile. I swear, I swear this isn't me, though who could possibly blame me if it was? If Eve can sleepwalk through life, why can't I be someone else one solitary night?

"So here's to you boys in rescue," I say, lifting my glass. Nothing to drink. I let it fall all the way down, shatter on the terrace. Now people are leaping to their feet and taking notice. I take the helmet and throw it at their smug, defensive faces. It hits the edge of an empty table and flips in a manic end-over-end and bounces along the ground. I say, "It wasn't a body, was it? You stuffed what was left in a garbage sack. It's all my wife's thought about since I got home." Eve claws at my arm. "Honey," I say. "Don't you want to stop wondering?"

She won't meet my eyes.

"My wife," I shout, "later she'll say I'm drunk, but I'm not even close. I'm trying to help her, but she'll say I'm a mess."

Eve slams her hand down on the rail. I look at her in time to see this: Eve, my wife, shattered one instant, put back together the next. Composed from shards. Weird, defying all laws of space and time, but in the blink of an eye we've relived our entire year, ever since Joey. Exhausted from holding the pieces together. Shattered when at rest.

She opens her purse and rifles for her wallet, her tissues, her compact, but takes nothing out, then fastens the clasp and adjusts the strap on her shoulder so the bag lays flat along the side of her hip. She turns and walks. I could see the stiffness a mile away, even in her clown clothes, willing herself to walk-not-run as she goes through the doors. The murmurs silence as the crowd parts for her, this group that used to know her.

I catch up in the parking lot and weave an arm through hers. The overhead lamps are coming to life one by one all over us. I can hear the waves from one way, the highway from the other. The headlights string along the hillside. I tell her, "No one ought to get blamed here.

All right? I'm just—I don't know. I'm making it up as I go along. I didn't mean to get carried away."

"You think you're so funny," she says, standing at the car door, looking out at the water. "You make things impossible."

"My conscience is clean, Eve."

She unlocks the door and gets behind the wheel and I stand at the passenger side, waiting. My colleagues and their wives jam the doors of the building, but I'm watching Eve every second through the curved glass. I rap on the window. I jiggle the handle. I say, "So you're leaving me? We get this far and you're going to leave me in a parking lot?"

In response, my wife starts the engine. People will have things to say about what happens next, and the question I'll put forth, professor I am: what's going to happen? What, really, are my options? Help would be appreciated. I am in need of answers, and I too am sick of wondering.

# PUPS

arry had to explain what they were: they seemed only puppies to Mollie—soft, needle-nosed, licky, a nest of energy on her lap. "They like you," he said, squatting on his haunches and clicking his tongue. One dashed for him, nails skittering across the patio. The other lowered his snout to sniff a circuitous trail. In a minute Barry had them both by the scruff. "They're wolves."

Mollie stopped brushing the shed fur off her jeans.

"Grays," said Barry.

Mollie's questions jammed in her throat. She watched him gripping the collars of two wild animals, leading them off the deck to the wire kennel he'd built. He pushed them in and closed the gate before they could bolt away. Inside they jumped at the cage, put their noses through the mesh, whimpered to be let out again.

"You'll get used to it," he said, to her or the animals. He washed under the outdoor spigot and then turned, wiping his hands dry on his shirt. The beard he was growing smudged his cheeks and chin—maybe it too could be removed with vigorous scrubbing. "Will you stop it? That look. Christ."

"This is my 'not a chance you're keeping wolves' look."

"I'm keeping them and eventually you'll forgive me."

"Sure of that, are you?" said Mollie, but was already coming up short for ways to influence the situation. What did she have left in her arsenal? Refuse to do his laundry. Stop speaking to him. Starve him for sex. It'd be another week at least before he ran out of clothes, the silent treatment was laughable considering he didn't listen, and as for sex, she figured he had better odds of knowing a hussy than he did going to a Laundromat. Mollie rubbed the back of her neck, suddenly tense. "How about I ask you, as a favor to me, please get rid of the goddamn things?"

"That was almost nice," he said. He poured himself a pint from the Mr. Beer tap and lowered into a chaise longue and looked across the way, admiring his new animals. Last spring it was remodeling the patio; this year, wolves; what about next spring? She tried to imagine the worst, but the wire fencing of the kennel rang out and scattered the coming-into-focus premonition of a sports car, a Marshall stack, a redhead college cheerleader. One wolf stood with its nose at the fence, ears perked and stare intent. The other paced an infinite pattern across the concrete slab Barry had spent last week forming, pouring, leveling. The neighbors must have wondered *what now?* No way they had imagined wolves, heads down to protect their throats, stalking.

"You're losing perspective here," Barry said. "How long have we been talking about getting pets? Just last week we were in agreement. You were all for it."

"I agreed to getting a *dog*—"

"—Technically they are dogs," he interrupted. "I got two of them, I know. Sorry about that."

Mollie forced herself to go slowly—speaking to her man-child, after all. "They are not pets. They are not domesticated. You can't sanely call them dogs. They're wild animals, Barry."

"Won't be wild for long." He wiped his mouth on his Henley sleeve and took another drink. He hadn't peeled his gaze from the caged, pacing animals. "Everything will be fine," he said. "Want to hear my name ideas?"

Mollie stormed into the house, overflowing with her own ideas of what he could call them.

In the kitchen she put water on to boil and got a mug out of the cabinet, grabbed the counter's lip to steady her shaking hands. Out the window the black walnut trees swayed. She loved the trees, how they opened like umbrellas over the house, but the kennel stood in the corner of her view, an eyesore, an irritant baiting her attention. One wolf then the other circled into and out of her sightline.

The kettle ticked, water spillage tissing as it evaporated in the burner's flame. She found the tea she wanted and dropped it in the dry mug, tag dangling over the side like an ornament. A dozen kinds of tea—that was her indulgence, fitting all on one shelf—not an outdoor beer tap or a boat docked at Millerton Lake or a new hunting rifle or murderous pets.

At first she'd supported Barry's new interest in the outdoors, even encouraged him to take hiking trips with his buddies. He worked all day in an office, poring over numbers, catching other people's mistakes. Mollie couldn't imagine more tedious work, so she bought him khaki shorts by North Face and a fleece Columbia vest and two hundred–dollar waterproof boots. Go and have fun, she used to tell him. Release your steam. She'd once felt a sting of pride seeing him stand over the bullet grill, stainless steel spatula in hand, his new fishing hat on his head ringed with a dozen brightly colored flies, cooking what he'd caught—but now? His shit had taken over the house and was spreading across the yard, from the outdoorsman magazines on the coffee table to the fire pit in the backyard. *Wolves*, she thought, killing the flame under the kettle, *moron*.

The phone rang as she was pulling out a dinette chair. Barry came inside and shut the door behind him. When the phone rang it was usually for him. Mollie couldn't think of five friends who had called her this year.

"Yo. Hey, Rands." He turned his back to write on the paper pad magnetized to the fridge. His voice loud, like a kid overacting in the school play. "Alright. Got it. See you." He hung up the phone. "That was Rands," he said.

"Do tell."

Barry ripped the sheet off the pad and creased it. "Are we starting down that road again? Sarcasm noon and night?" He paused, but Mollie didn't answer. "I know why you're mad," he said.

"Congratulations, detective."

"They're exactly like dogs at this age. Pups."

"Right, I've heard that they don't get a taste for blood until the teenage years."

"Not if you domesticate as puppies," he said. "This is what I've been trying to tell you. The guy said you teach them obedience, how to walk on a leash, a few tricks, things like that, and they'll grow up to be just big, gorgeous dogs."

"This is what the wolf dealer guy told you."

He creased the paper a final time. "Fine. You know what? I've got packing to do." He started for the hallway. "Maybe you'll listen when I get back."

"You're not going anywhere until you make this right."

"Rands said the fish are practically jumping into the boat. That's why he called. I'm going."

"They're your *puppies*. Not mine. If you go, take them with you. See how Rands likes it."

He cocked his head, looking so weary that Mollie thought he might wilt to the linoleum. "Taking them on the lake would not be domesticating. And I don't have time for this. I'll write out what to do for you."

"Now who's not listening?" she said, sipping her tea, calmer somehow—placid with resolve that if Barry goes, she'll let them die. She would. Raising wolves wasn't among her wifely duties.

———

His steps came down the hallway. She'd been hearing the scrape of hangers on the rod, the closet door slamming shut. Now Mollie watched him drop his duffel by the front door, select a ring of keys from the hooks hanging on the sideboard, pat himself for his wallet, his cellular, his fishing boat cigars. He scanned the room for things he might need, careful not to see her sitting at the nook.

"Short notice this time," she said. "Getting shorter all the time, huh?"

He shrugged.

"That rascally Rands," she said. She'd never met this nature boy of his and believed more and more that the real name might be Roxanne, maybe, or Rachel. The pinched, glowering face Barry wore was, for now, confirmation enough. She wasn't in a hurry to watch his excuse-making contortionist act, or to have forgiveness tricked out of her when he finally broke down and confessed to everything: the infidelity, the pile of white lies, promising in the end to be a better man. He was right: she would eventually forgive him, for the wolves and the bimbos, unless she was careful.

"I left feeding instructions on the dresser," he said, picking his bag from the floor. It banged against his calves following him out the door.

Mollie refused to offer him even a parting nod.

"See you Sunday," he called through the last, closing gap.

His Silverado started and idled in the drive. He appeared to Mollie as a silhouette behind the wheel, arranging something in the passenger seat. Behind him children rode bikes, scooters, roller-skated in the cul-de-sac, the helmets they wore curved like full tummies. When they had first moved in she couldn't believe this was her neighborhood, these rambling houses built according to a cattle rancher's sense of space. Their money went a long way in Caruthers, a small town twenty miles south of Fresno. She'd felt rich living out here. Their house was the largest on the block, built on a country-sized lot. They spent two years making improvements, toying with the idea of children, slowly letting that idea fade into the background. What happened? Barry could never quite see himself as a father, less so now that he wanted to spend every weekend fishing, hiking, camping. Mollie wasn't one of those girls who picked baby names at first menstruation, so being childless didn't horrify her.

That was her thinking before the empty house, before Rands, before wolves.

Barry honked his horn and the children playing behind him scattered to the sidewalks. He backed into the street too fast, a tantrum, one last gesture meant to guilt her. Who needed children, married to a man like that? She could still see his shape in the cab, holding the phone to his ear and steering away with one hand. Even in his acting-out he remained predictable, too absorbed with his own intricate fantasy to know what he was telling the world: I'm up to my lures in a midlife crisis. Mollie found it his least-attractive phase yet, and the guilt trip aimed her way hit her as something else, something baleful and urgent and as yet un-translated.

She went around turning on lamps and closing all the curtains, switched on the television and flipped the channels until she found a rerun of the show with creepy death—glowing skeletons, modern-era mummies, corpses pulled out of cold waters. All in all it was a terrible show, but she liked the man and woman solving crimes together, his instinctual reactions against her strict adherence to process and reason, no matter how fantastical the case. He lent his strength to protect her, even though she obviously didn't need protecting, and Mollie liked that old-fashioned devotion in a man as much as she did a woman of independence. During a commercial she fixed herself carrot sticks and spinach dip, a leftover (hardly touched) appetizer from one of Barry's grill-outs, and then hunkered into the couch with a lap quilt and one too many pillows.

Daydreaming through the familiar TV episode, the team was called to her backyard, where a pair of reeking canine corpses had been discovered in an unearthed cage. The man lobbied that they take the case on grounds that whoever would kill two dogs in a kennel was a step away from killing a human being, while she, the rock of logic, shook her brilliant, stubborn, pretty head.

*They're wolves, she said. They're not dogs.*

*Dogs are dogs, okay.*

*That's not true. There are significant evolutionary and social differences.*

*Social differences. In dogs.*

*Not dogs, wolves. Wolves move in packs while domesticated dogs are bred to be companions for humans. A pack is no longer important to them, while wolves separated from the larger group would feel ostracized and might react with aggression and quite possibly with the intent to kill. The predatory instinct would be subverted by a host of reactions, from blind rage to killing a victim as an offering to the pack to gain re-admittance.*

*You're saying whoever killed these dogs was defending herself?*

*I'm saying that whoever separated them from the pack in the first place put himself and his loved ones in serious danger and clearly had a brain the size of a cashew.*

Mollie laughed at her self-indulgence, kicking off the quilt and almost spilling the television tray. She could write for this show, only a matter of moving to Hollywood and submitting a sample. The interview would be a snap: yes, of course she subscribed to the notion people never change—everyone is the same person this week as last. Wasn't she herself proof of that?

Outdoors they were barking, banging against the cage.

Mollie went to the slider and tried to look out. The porch light glared back at her. She turned it off and brought her face right to the glass, her breath fogging a patch; spring rain was falling. The new metal posts of the kennel seemed to shine, the wire mesh stretched between like a net. She squinted her eyes for a trace of movement, or a pair of bright eyes reflecting back at her. Had they gotten out? Had Barry done such a crap job erecting the structure that it failed the first day? Then a gray side appeared within the cage. Four legs. They were in there circling. Stalking a puddle in the depressed center of the concrete floor. Her eyes were adjusting to the dark. Mollie watched them rotate in and out of view, yellow-gray coats spiked, the fur darkest along the watershed of their spines. They went with their heads down, but their snouts didn't track the ground. Their postures looked more like travelers bent against the rain than predators tracking prey. A sad scene, watching them go over the same ground with no other path available. And yet she was too nervous to turn her back on them, even with the cage and the glass and the open space between them. She took a few steps back and closed the curtain.

Mollie must have visited fifty web pages before she was willing to go outside. The room was too dark to read the list she'd made. When she'd first logged on, she only wanted answers to a few questions: 1) do they howl at night? 2) how fast do they grow? and 3) in what specific ways am I in danger?

They could creep on their paws like cats, rocket at you with bullet-like suddenness, and a pack of wolves could prey upon animals much larger than they were individually, but did two count as a pack? Not technically, she inferred, but hadn't she been told that very morning they were technically mere dogs? A German shepherd, that was a dog. Black Lab, dog. Bloodhound, obviously. The Internet confirmed that the animals caged in the backyard could harm her, would soon be large enough to kill her, and in fact could howl quite lustily. *Dog* was an inadequate term. Wolves possessed sharp eyesight, could distinguish color, able to read every shiver or tick that passed through its prey. Their sense of smell was highly tuned; they could tell one animal from another by scents on the wind; they coded odors the way humans remember faces. Wolves could be aggressive, and were always unpredictable. She copied down warning signs and ways she might protect herself. Did this make her paranoid or practical? Was she being smart or acting scared? Barry accused her of detail freak-ness, but under these circumstances gathering details seemed only prudent. He was an asshole for leaving her with them. She was sure Google would prove it if she entered the search parameters, "total+shithead."

Mollie turned on the hall light on her way to the bedroom. She needed to hide her notes. It was the kind of thing Barry liked to use against her, whether he was accusing her of being a slob *(Post-its! Post-its everywhere!)*, getting old *(Why must you write everything down, Nana?)*, or not supporting him *(It's like your purpose in life is to refute me, like it's just so hard to trust my knowledge on the subject)*. She folded the papers and buried them in a drawer with her panties, one of the places Barry wouldn't go. The stained crotches from leaky tampons and other minor accidents repelled him, never mind that she handled his dirties with their odors and happy trails and weird slots without a word of complaint.

As she closed the drawer she saw the list Barry had left for her. His handwriting slanted the wrong way, a righty writing like a lefty, his sweaty palm smudging the words:

> Steps for Feeding Bartles and James (our babies)
>
> 1. Open bag of food you'll find in laundry room
> 2. Go outside to the cage, henceforth referred to as "the kennel"
> 3. Open kennel gate with key, which you'll find where the keys go, marked "kennel"
> 4. Go inside kennel
> 5. Firmly but lovingly tell B and J to stop jumping while at the same time…
> 6. You CLOSE kennel gate behind you (this is IMPORTANT!)
> 7. Pour food into bowls, one for each pup
> 8. Change drinking water of course
> 9. Take a goddamn minute to enjoy the rewards of pet ownership
> 10. Go out through the gate and lock the gate from the outside WITHOUT letting them escape into our fuddy-duddy neighborhood

Mollie wadded it up. Threw it at the bathroom wastebasket as she walked past the open door, missed, let it sit there on the floor behind the toilet where it belonged, and then she didn't know what to do, where to go. Maybe call her sister in Oregon, let her know she was packing a few things and was on her way. But Mollie would hear how she'd been wrong and Delia had *always* been right. She wouldn't call her sister; she wouldn't leave this house she loved, this *fuddy-duddy* neighborhood. It was a question of what to do with the wolves, and of how to put them to use.

Mollie applied generous doses of perfume to her wrists and to the spots behind her ears and to her chest where the collar closed. For now, her hair in a rough, loose ponytail would do. She didn't bother to try and flatten the waves her curls made on the top of her head. Didn't care that flyways snarled the nape of her neck and caught the bright bathroom light like smoke. Who cared, right then, that her roots were gray once more? If any of the neighbors were spying they'd only see a woman feeding her new pets in her own backyard, nothing devious in that. And was her plan so devious? It seemed to Mollie that she was merely returning serve, so to speak. Meeting one act with another. Letting her husband know that at last he'd found her limits.

She opened the glass slider. Drizzle tapped the aluminum patio awning but the real rain had passed. Steam slithered in the grass. Broken branches, combs of pine needles, clumps of lichen littered the yard. She breathed mouthfuls of thick air and tried to stop her heart from pounding. The wolves—the *pups*, she told herself—stood with their snouts at the kennel gate, looking at her. Waiting, she imagined, for a chance to attack. No, they're caged, for god's sake, they're *puppies*. Hadn't they licked her face that morning? She'd watched too much television, received an overdose of macabre close-ups, absorbed too many sentimental, righteous motivations. They're puppies, harmless, babies. Approaching the gate, Mollie bent at the waist, kissing her lips and cooing, her hands clasped together to arrest the shakes. The pups danced on their paws, tails wagging their hindquarters, panting through sly grins. She unlocked the gate and tried to fill the opening with her body, pushing them back with her knee. She closed the gate behind her. She petted their heads, let them sniff and lick her hands, singing to them, "Good dogs, good boys, my puppies." Once she believed they didn't intend to chew off a finger, she settled herself down cross-legged on the kennel floor. The concrete felt cold through her jeans. "Is this why you pace?" she said. "Because the floor?" In answer the two pups vied for position on her lap, bathing her face with kisses and pressing their sides against her. "Good boys, down now, that's good, my good boys."

Were they boys? Whoever heard of a female wolf? Weren't all wolves male, prowling and sharp-sensed for weakness?

Mollie scratched their nape, scratched their sides, scratched the tops of their heads between the pert ears, let her hand be played between their teeth, those teeth, teeth she'd read not an hour earlier were meant for ripping meat from the bone. Eye to cold eye with the beasts, their pets, the pups, her wolves. She fed them. Watered them. Stood outside the kennel as they ate: "You're my boys, yes you are, you're my big, bad wolves." Their tales wagged at the sound of her singsong voice. "Goodnight, my boys, goodnight," she called from the slider door.

Inside she went straight to the bathroom. She turned the shower to just below scalding and washed her hair, scrubbed every inch of her skin, and then let the water run over her. Her shoulders quaked under the spray, her sobs were masked in the water's hiss, and every trace of wolves or tears swirled down the drain.

She shut the water off, reached through the steam and found Barry's towel on the rack and patted herself off before stepping onto the mat and drying off. The shallow knap burnished her skin, scraping rather than absorbing moisture. She could smell his body wash, his dandruff shampoo, the stale alcohol scent of his aftershave lotion. She wrapped his towel, short and narrow, around her as best she could, and went down the hall to their bedroom. Mollie rooted in the dirty clothes hamper, pulling out a pair of his dungarees, his polo shirt, a dirty pair of his socks and underwear. All Barry's. She pulled them on layer-by-layer, cinching the trousers with one of his work belts and letting the shirt hem fall down over it. Even the collar seemed to rise too high, scuffing her ears. But it covered her, that's what she wanted: to be fully encased in Barry, to become Barry for anyone, anything that saw or smelled. In the living room she put on a windbreaker he left on the back of the dinette chair. She zipped it to her chin. The elastic sleeves cut across her palms. She could draw her fingers inside, as if into protective shells. The too-large hood came down her brow, and she cinched the strings to make a portal just large enough for her eyes, nose, and mouth. In the hall mirror she could barely see her own shower-scrubbed cheeks.

She felt shrunken inside her husband's clothes. Maybe she wouldn't fool anyone she passed on the street, but what about the animals in her backyard? Were his smells from the hamper ripe enough to fool wolves? She laced his boots by the door, where he always left them, pulling them tight over her ankles while her feet slipped inside. She wasn't sure she could walk in the things. Every step forward her feet slid. Concentrate, she told herself: a few minutes of cruelty, that's all you need to accomplish; be the moron, be the asshole, do it silently, let his odors speak for themselves.

She took slow, klutzy steps toward the kennel. The boot treads seemed to stick in the damp grass. More like Barry than Barry, she thought, and the next moment doubted she could fool a moth with this act. The wolves had come to the gate, panting, wolf-smiling, wagging. Their senses cut through her disguise—no, they were stupid animals, more gullible than children. Look at them, hopping around as if they think they'll be let out. She stopped in her tracks. It took a few seconds to overcome their energy, but the wolves too grew calm. They began to stalk back and forth, heads lowered, eyes trained on Mollie, or Barry—whomever, whatever now loomed outside the wire walls.

In the grass was a length of deadwood shed from the tree. She picked it up, hands pulled inside the windbreaker sleeves, and wielded it like a club, approaching the kennel with it raised to strike. Their pacing stopped. Their jugulars protected, they looked up at her. Mollie was making them cower before Barry.

With all her strength she brought it down on the cage. The stick broke, and the metal rang in Mollie's ears. The wolves pressed themselves into the far corner to escape her, him, this. She used what was left of the stick, a handle not much longer than her two stacked fists, to rake across the wire, going the length of one wall, turning the corner and going down another, around and around, chasing the wolves until they hunkered together in the middle. She stabbed the stick through the holes, overturning their empty food dishes, spilling their water bowls. All without letting a sound pass from her mouth, not a shout, not a laugh, not a whimper. She was not herself.

Barry's alarm blared talk radio. Mollie put her feet on the floor, used to winter cold shocking her awake, but the boards were pleasant, a little cool, spring boards. Sunday. She silenced the alarm. His clothes lay in a rumpled pile at the foot of the bed, windbreaker, boots, and all. That she'd been able to sleep surprised her, but in fact she'd gone under within seconds of her head hitting the pillow, hair still damp, hands still numb from the sting of violence. The wolves, she double-checked through the curtain, were stalking in their cage, looking no different than before Barry had frightened them.

In the kitchen she poured herself a bowl of cereal, listening to a neighbor's car go down the street. When she was growing up, Mollie had been forced by her mother to attend Sunday Mass, while her father demanded family vacations every summer, to Yellowstone, to Yosemite, to Glacier Park. She remembered sticking to the vinyl seats, the sun muted through the dirty glass of their Ford van, the AC too weak to reach her, while in the front seat her mother wore a cardigan and her proud father's bare arms riffled with gooseflesh. None of her brothers or sisters were ever comfortable in the van; they all compromised and suffered. Mollie was one of the nebulous middle kids, not the trusted oldest or the adored youngest, without the obvious talents her nearest siblings on either side had—for piano, for soccer—that distinguished them in their parents' minds. Mollie was the dreamer, and felt that she compromised and suffered more than the rest. She resented church. Hated being dragged down highways for days at a time with nothing but bathroom breaks at horrifying rest stops and crowded motel rooms. She dreamed herself far away, the beloved nucleus of some other family, or later, married to an understanding man. Now she drew back the kitchen curtains to watch the wolves stalking. Her own faint reflection was waiting for her in the glass. She had finally distinguished herself as the daughter who moved far away. College out of state, a marriage to a man her parents didn't meet until the rehearsal dinner, two visits home in the last ten years. Spent her whole childhood chafing as a sister and daughter, and now she felt alone.

Mollie stomped down the hall to the bedroom, her steps seeming to shake the whole empty house, and changed, cinching the sweatshirt hood so it covered her chin and her forehead. A neighbor could glance over the fence and think it was her husband.

She crossed the lawn, dew darkening the toes of Barry's boots, and unwound the garden hose behind her. She threaded on the nozzle used for washing the car. Already the wolves seemed alert in their pacing, unwilling to take their eyes from her except for the fraction of a second needed to turn their heads. As she approached they kept toward the back fence, but not yet growling, not yet baring fangs. She stopped walking a few feet from the kennel. She let the breeze drag across her clothes, and she watched the wolves work their noses in the air.

Then she turned the nozzle on them. The stream sliced the wires, hitting the sides of the wolves hard. They leapt against the back wall, wire ringing out. At first they moved together and the spray followed. Next they separated, one burying itself in a corner while Mollie—while Barry—focused his water torture on the other. It let out a piercing cry, an animal's cry that might have been a child's cry. Would that bring out the neighbors? Would that open the blind eye of their neighborhood? That all of this was happening in secret, yet out in the daylight, thrilled her venomously. She made Barry give the wolves one more blast. Then turned off the water at the spigot. Rolled up the hose. Went indoors, trying to dry her hands on the front of his damp sweatshirt.

Mollie showered and sorted the laundry and started a load of clothes, darks. She heard more family cars taking to the road, heading for any of the dozen late-morning protestant services, but otherwise only a deep, amplifying quiet. She sat before the vanity mirror and applied makeup as carefully as she would have for a night out. Worked at camouflaging the talons at the corners of her eyes, blending away the white scar on her chin, the new blemish at her hairline. She tidied her eyebrows. Plucked two gray, stray hairs from her neck. She bleached the down on her upper lip. Brushed and curled and sprayed her hair so that it grazed the tops of her shoulders when she turned her head. Perfume, Cristalle, same scent she'd worn yesterday. Finally she dressed in fresh clothes from her closet. Would they smell him on her? Did something of Barry survive the cleansing? A moment when her clean clothes touched his dirties—all the horrible things that could happen when she entered that kennel! And yet she had to go. She had to show the difference between them.

Broiling clouds were stretched across the sky, drawn by a cold wind. She hadn't taken four steps away from the slider before she noticed the wolves shivering, literally trembling, their unnerving wolf grins miserable, their strong bodies so soaked they'd been emasculated.

She retrieved clean towels from the linen closet. They had been laundered recently; only she had touched them, when folding, straight from the dryer. She put them under her arm and went back out, unlocked the kennel, ducked inside. On hands and knees she dried the wolves, a fine spray of water sloughed from their fur, their fey pup-coats regaining mass. They crawled into her lap, dampened her clothes, chilled her until she too was fighting the shivers. Saving them from the wet and the cold, from the thoughtless brute who'd brought them here to abuse them, from abandonment among strangers—the worst punishment she'd yet experienced, abandonment among strangers.

And they were reciprocating. They made her feel less alone. Doing what pets were supposed to do: make your heart sing, help you sacrifice a part of yourself for the good of another living thing. Yet as their coats filled out some of her fear returned. She didn't belong here. These were not mere pups—Christ, she wanted nothing to do with them, but those infant blue eyes—she could almost see her reflection multiplied in their shine.

He came home late that night. Mollie was already in bed, the house locked up tight, dark. She heard his key in the deadbolt, then his steps, his hands feeling the wall for a light switch, then saw the sweep of light under the bedroom door. She followed his sounds room to room:

washing hands in the bathroom, emptying his bladder into the toilet in a hard stream, flushing, washing his hands again, splashing his face… the loose mount of the towel rack rattled in the wall between them, and he groaned stiffly sitting on the throne to pull off his boots, and the boots scuffed the wall as he tossed them aside. She'd been living so long with him that every sound had a corresponding action, every action a particular cast of face, every face telltale of a mood. Mollie already knew, for example, he'd rouse her for sex when he entered the bedroom because she'd heard him take a clean washrag from the linen closet.

The door opened and closed. She could feel him standing at the foot of the bed, searching the hills of blankets for a sign she was awake—not that it would matter. He'd start tugging at her clothes as if pulling her from sleep, see her cheeks flush with dreaming and mistake it for desire. "Moll-doll," he whispered, climbing onto the bed. "Mollie Hend-ricks," he was singing, voice filling. God how he smelled of dirty fish and stale cigars and the ripeness of lake water, of outboard exhaust, grill smoke, dribbled beer. He pulled down the blanket and took hold of her shoulder, then guided himself into position behind her as if docking a boat, his hand sliding into her tank top. "Guess who's home?" he breathed into her ear.

"You're waking me up," she said.

He kissed her neck, tried to suck off an earlobe.

He'd only been gone two nights—when he stayed home, four or five nights would pass without putting a hand on her. Was he making up for being gone, or for the company he kept out there?

"Come on, daddy's home," he said, rolling her hips to the mattress, getting on top. He was already naked; that odor was coming from him, his skin, his pores, his hair, his mouth. He was pushing the panties aside with his hand, going in through the leg hole of her shorts, and then he broke inside and was working in her, these small, dry thrusts. "I missed you," he said, all breath, up on his elbows. "Tell me you missed me."

The wetness was starting, and it wasn't hurting as much. Her first time had hurt awfully, and her sisters said that was normal, when she fessed up one night in their shared room. Every time gets better, her nearest elder, Delia the athlete, had ventured, and it never hurts again. She'd never felt closer to her sisters than during this exchange, every word bearing the weight of confession and the welcome-bells of adulthood. Mollie had savored that advice for a year, until the next time she let it happen, another neighborhood boy—*it never hurts again*. But this hurt. Her husband hurts her. Every sign she threw his way, lying still, unreciprocating, her pinched face, her bent lips, the eyes squeezed against tears and then the tears themselves, nothing stopped him. To him, the tears she shed were for kissing away. Little invitations for tenderness.

"Come to me," he moaned.

"Not inside me."

"Mollie—"

He arched his back, lifted his trembling chin, and groaned in relief. "God I missed you," he said, falling off.

"You're such an asshole."

"Moll-doll," he said.

She rolled away from him, holding in the sobs and screams and names she wanted to hurl forth. Everything, she assured herself, would soon be revealed. For the first time she had a plan.

He was up early the next morning, alarm clock blaring for work, and she let him rise and eat breakfast and read his sports headlines alone. Swaddled in the covers, a pleasant warmth covering her, she once more followed his routines remotely, seeing in her mind's eye. He opened the slider and clapped his hands on the patio, talking at the wolves like one might a Pop Warner team. There was nothing between his words. No barking, no growls that she heard. She waited for the kennel gate to preen on its hinges, but that didn't happen, either. A little enthusiasm had been leeched from his voice when he said, "What's the matter, it's me, you guys, it's your Papa." That was all. Nothing revealed today. He left for work without shouting goodbye.

She pulled herself out of bed a few hours later, sore, the bed's warmth overheated, under her skin now like a fever. Mollie repeated the ritual: dressed as Barry, smelling like Barry, she tormented the wolves. At first they seemed unsure what was happening. They'd learned nothing. Wolf-grins stretched on their panting mouths, pleading. It took time for their lips to curl back from white teeth, their eyes to dial into points, to volley warning growls and full-throated barks that shot through the town. She struck the wire fencing hard enough for her hands to sting, her ears to be left ringing. Soon her rage won out against the pups' threatening show, and she made them cower, whimper, curl into pill bug–like coils and wait for it to end. Maybe she was disappointed in them. Their venom drained too quickly, their teeth holstered too soon. Growl, bark, let out that rage! You'll grow into wolves! What then will you have to fear from him?

After a shower, after grabbing a bite to eat from the depleted fridge, Mollie went outside to comfort them. She unlocked the kennel gate and entered the cage. She squatted on her haunches and clicked her tongue. They lifted their heads, ears tented, eyes—those eyes—focusing on her, sharpening.

These wolves recognized her face.

And yet they came to her and let themselves be petted and talked to. One of them, sighing, rested his jaw on her thigh, eyes looking toward the walls of the house. It was empty. Nothing, not even the hand of a clock, was moving. No more threats would emerge from inside.

Mollie wondered what a pup could see in a stone-dead house. *A wolf, when separated from the pack, will fall back on its most basic instincts to survive.* Had she read that? Invented it as rationale for what she was doing? Or did it come to her to explain something else? Why Barry needed to own these killers. Why Mollie would remain here to raise them.

# THE RULES

They load handsaws, axes, and splitting wedges into the truck bed, putting in last their jack saw with the rusted blade and cracked, gray handles, then cover the load with a tarp, the middle sagging already with the weight of a sloppy snow. Cal is dressed for a long day in the woods, wool coat and work boots, canvas gloves tucked in his back pocket. These last desolate months he had refused to leave the house. Torn jeans and undone flannel shirts. Bare gut stitched with hair. He let the garden die under the frost and left the grocery runs to his fourteen-year-old son, Marty, who learned to guide their old Toyota Scout down the rutted back roads and corkscrewing highways to Mariposa. Now Cal takes the corners too fast. Marty feels the tires lose and find their grip, moments like free fall between jolting traction.

Around Midpines, Cal pulls the Scout off the road and Marty gets out to lock the hubs into four-wheel, the first breath of cold a relief after being trapped in the heated cab. He looks up the old logging trail, thick with overhung boughs and melting slush before disappearing into the falling snow. He turns back to Cal. His graying ponytail hangs serpentine over one shoulder and his lips pout under his beard. He gulps coffee from a gourd, eyes bolted straight ahead. Marty's gaze slides to the empty place next to him where Mom should have been. She had worked fiendishly alongside his father, as if defending this life she'd chosen for them all, bucking fallen trees for a living. They had grown their own food and built all the pens corralling the mule team without cutting down a tree, without spending a cent. Sustaining themselves and the forest, she had said, completing the circle, protecting.

Cal lays on the horn and Marty jumps.

"You freeze to death out there?" Cal shouts through a slit in the window.

Marty folds his gloves into his hip pocket. His palms are red and damp, the snow such a thin mix of sludge that it has soaked through the canvas.

"This trail's going to be death," he says, climbing back in.

Cal guides the truck into the soggy tire ruts.

"Tomorrow the sun will be out," Cal says. "We'll be able to work with our shirts off. It'll feel great, Marty. You watch."

Frosted pastures open up out the window, running toward sheer granite faces and steep, tree-covered slopes, then thick stands of pines close the view once again. Cal stops and points to a giant redwood lying like a wall at the edge of a clearing, tall enough to make a snow shadow on the leeward side. They inspect the break point, a jagged spire in the air. No black crusts the edges, so it didn't fall from a lightning strike, but from being too old, too big.

"This is the biggest fall we've seen yet," says Cal.

He walks the perimeter, estimating its length, pausing long at the broken trunk, the annual rings.

"It will take months to get this bad boy pieced up."

He checks the low sun, guesses the time.

"We'll cut for a couple days, then use the team to bring it down, by the book."

Marty digs out the small handsaws from under the tarp. The handles are black and smooth from their palms. Marty hands one to Cal, loosens the wing nut on his own, opens the blade. For most of the afternoon they work the small branches high up the shaft. The cutting is easy, some of the wood snapping off with the blade only halfway through, but the snow soaks them, weighs them down. The sky remains dark, the clouds overhead a close, thick purple. Marty's stomach growls, his sawing arm trembles with exertion, and his jaw hurts from clamping together. Marty stops, listens. His father isn't cutting, either.

Cal stands away from the tree, staring at it.

"I hate this," he says. "It's spring. It's supposed to be sunshine and sunflowers. Look," he says, gesturing across the buried pasture, "this should all be yellow, dancing in the wind. All this white hurts my eyes."

"Tomorrow we'll work with our shirts off," says Marty, straining toward the baritone of his father's voice.

Cal regards him coldly.

"I'm glad I amuse you."

Marty looks at his boots.

"Let's get back to work," says Cal.

Marty helps drag out the jack saw. He loved it as a kid, when the work was too big for him. He'd lose his feet and be jostled back and forth, laughing, a kind of teeter-totter, and Cal's old joke that if he pulled hard, Marty's thin body would slide through the cut. When Mom helped, their weight together became a counterbalance to Cal's on the other side, the teeth humming through the grain. Now Marty can match him alone and it's not fun anymore.

They start the teeth into the trunk, cutting lengthwise from the break to a place in the middle. In an hour they've gone less than a foot into the slab. His palms throb inside his gloves. When the saw binds, Marty falls back into the snow and he stays down. The sky above him swells black.

"Back to work."

Cal tosses down his jacket.

"I'm taking a break."

"Wait until we're six more inches in."

"Now."

"If we rest every hour, we'll be up here for the rest of our lives."

Cal stands over him, hand out. Marty works up to an elbow.

"I was thinking that was your plan," he says.

Cal scans the tree, from the tip down the wide trunk, the saw sunk into the wood. He removes his gloves and beats them on his thigh.

"We'll work on the branches a while."

"That's not a break."

He walks away, leaving Marty in the snow.

"Get up now, son," he says.

Marty unfolds the saw to its boomerang curve and works away from his father. He peels his glove off to see if his palm has turned bloody, but the skin's only pink, creased with his grip. Still, it's easier than slicing into the core. The jack saw remains stalled in the wood, the handles drooping like broken wings. No one lives this way anymore, handsaws and mule teams, suffocating principles. But look at him, thinks Marty. Lording over a kingdom that's mostly gone, that was never really his. It's controlling him now. It threatens to steal Marty, too, demanding so much of his sweat and muscle that there will be nothing left once the fallen tree is sawdust and a bald slice of earth.

"Let's get back to the big boy," says Cal.

"A drink of water first."

"No. Six more inches."

"Who are you shitting, anyway?" says Marty. "We're never getting this tree out of here by ourselves."

Cal faces him, the open saw dangling from his hand.

"If your mother was here, she'd keel over, hearing you talk."

"If Mom was here we could get the job done."

Marty licks his lips, spits away from his feet. Cal tries to return to the tree but his hands are shaking.

"Fucking Jesus Christ," he roars, rearing up like a bear and casting away the saw.

It cuts through the air and buries itself in the snow and Cal turns hard to face down his son.

Marty squares to meet him, saw gripped like a dagger. The two have the same hazel eyes and cut jaws that jut forward when they're angry, teeth grinding, biting the rims of their lips. They stand more than an arm's reach away, but a lunge could fix that, even the smallest step and they'd be locked together, grappling.

They stand a few breaths, relaxing together slowly, turning away to scan the tundra for the saw.

"Find it for me, will you, Marty? I'm—just get it," he says, leaning against the trunk.

It's snowing harder, the footfalls deepening. He reaches the place the saw should be and kicks at the snow, but sees only white. Cal starts pounding toward him, but stops when he evens with the truck. He disappears behind the toolbox lid and then lifts out something Marty can't yet see.

"That is *not* by the book," says Marty when he gets back to the truck.

Cal is gassing up a chainsaw.

"Get away from me," he says.

Snow touches the shiny plastic shell, the links of the new blade.

"We can buck it up right, Dad. We'll find the saw—"

"I said go, Marty."

He looks at the fallen tree, the trunk shaved of branches.

"This snow will melt," he says. "We can come back with the team."

"It'd take us a year to get anything small enough for a mule to carry. You were right. Congratulations."

Cal pulls three times on the rope before the engine catches, the exhaust bluing in the cold. He revs it a few times, the thing screeching between them.

While Cal lays into the tree, Marty drags away the branches and cuts the biggest on the Scout tailgate. The chainsaw roars, echoing off the mountainsides and rattling in the trees. Cal's got one foot propped on the trunk. His shoulders are drawn tight against the saw, pushing it deeper. Marty can smell the sweetness of redwood, almost feel the soggy resistance it gives a blade.

"Dad," he shouts. "Let me spot you awhile."

Cal pulls up on the chainsaw and walks around the tree.

"Show me how to use it."

Cal shakes his head.

"This is too much saw for you."

He draws a deep breath, stretches his back, faces the trunk. He sinks the chainsaw into the wood again, but withdraws and lets it idle.

"You know your mother sends money?"

"No."

"Five hundred bucks worth of guilt every month. I hoard it away."

"That's good," says Marty. "Right?"

"We made a life for ourselves out here, exactly the kind she wanted, and then one day she accuses me of running away from the world. Like that was suddenly a crime."

Cal looks to his son.

"This chainsaw is technically yours. I used the guilt money. I thought, what the hell? The rules have changed."

"Let's work the jack saw," says Marty. "Let's do it right."

Cal shakes his head. The chain spins, chews into the trunk in a spray of dust and chips. Marty feels the splinters stinging his cheeks and turns away, then the sound changes. The engine stalls, pulls at Cal, almost ripping itself from his hands. The blade revs back to life and finds its way into Cal's foot.

Marty goes to him. The canvas top of his boot's split, soaking red. He palms his father's forehead and looks into his stony eyes, wide and dry.

"Dad, Jesus."

"It's numb, Marty."

"I'm getting you to a hospital."

"Do you hear what I'm saying? I can't feel it."

Marty moves down to the tear. He pries open the smiling gash in the boot to the cut, an angry bite taken from the slope, gushing with blood. Marty packs the foot with snow, pressing fistfuls down into the split.

He helps Cal to his feet. He's unsteady, the wounded leg dragging, and the ground is slick. They fall twice, three times, and Marty lands with his head on his father's chest. Above the trees, the horizon is the color of aluminum.

Cal shakes his son.

"Marty, get up now. I don't want to die out here."

Marty's eyes open. Together they rise, and he doesn't know if he's carrying Cal's weight or being lifted in his arms. The imprint they leave behind is unrecognizable, four legs, two spread arms, a bloody hole burned into the snow.

Marty drives the truck down the trail, the headlights cutting cones through the storm. He keeps his father awake as night closes in. They reach Mariposa, and Marty waits in a freezing room while Cal is stitched closed. Cal shows his son the butterfly sutures and Marty drives them back to their trailer.

That night, Cal uses a hammer to crack walnuts, rolled to the table in the rented hospital wheelchair. He bangs on the pointed tip of shells and scatters fragments across the room. The bits he can reach he saves in a coffee can. Marty feels each hammer crack in his knees, exhausted but not wanting his father to stay awake alone.

"Most people use nutcrackers," he says.

Cal puts down his instrument, crosses his arms, leans back.

"We have hammers," says Cal.

He rolls the chair back and looks at the pinkish bandage on his foot. His hair tangles down his shoulders, stripes of gray in dirty blonde. His skin is ashen and eyes glassy from the painkillers.

"It's still snowing. Can you believe that? What a shit year this has been," he says.

Marty comes to the table and brushes shell fragments into his palm and empties them in the trash.

"I forgot to check the team. I need to do that."

"You haven't forgotten those mules since you were eight years old," says Cal.

"Weird day," says Marty, buttoning his houndstooth coat over his chest.

The cold stings his face, burrows up his sleeves. The moonlight is oily on the snow. He hears the team moving in the pen, sees their blue shapes taking form beyond the rail fence. Of course he had remembered to water them, to lay out the feed and to stow the empty sacks before dark. The mules shuffle indifferently as he approaches. He steps up on the first rail and leans his elbows over the fence and whistles. Their heads turn his way and then shake his presence off as if escaping a fly.

"Get your rest," he whispers. "You've got a mother of a big tree to haul down."

Marty steps off the fence. He can see Cal through the window, cradling his head, elbows propped on the table's edge.

"Get your rest," he says again, this time sure he means it.

# TURNING OVER

If Barger had found her sleeping in the middle of the bed when they first married (eight years come May), he would have grazed her cheek with the back of his finger and then kissed her, a kiss that would have lifted her up off the sheets and deposited her like a feather on her side. Tonight he took hold of her shoulder and shook.

Sandy uncurled herself. Straightening legs, stretching arms, pointing chin, making a goddamn production out of turning over. "How was your walk?" she mumbled.

Barger sat on the bed and unlaced his shoes. "Like putting one foot in front of the other."

"I had such a funny dream," she said. "I think you woke me from it so it didn't finish. You want to hear it?"

"What. Now?"

"You're not even ready for bed."

Barger peeled off his pants and shirt and climbed between the sheets.

"You're not going to brush your teeth?"

"I haven't eaten anything for hours and I've given my teeth a thorough rinsing." He swept his tongue from molar to molar. Barely a trace of the beer he'd glazed over with two cough drops and five laps around the block.

Sandy sat up, crossing her legs and adjusting her nightgown over her knees. Her bedside lamp came on. "You're not even going to change out of your shorts?" She gathered a corner of sheet and rolled it between her hands. Then Barger knew he wouldn't get to sleep after all. There was something weighing on her and if she didn't unburden her soul tonight tears would come tomorrow without any real reason, except for this hollow feeling, here, right behind the sternum. "Remember Wink?" she said. "I dreamed about Wink just now."

Barger remembered. The potato-sized, crippled bunny Sandy had tried to nurse to health when they were dating. It was the runt of the litter and its front paw was folded to the shape of an almond. When the mother moved the nest two days after birthing she left him behind. Wink slept twenty hours a day, and would have slept right into oblivion without intervention. Thank God Sandy was there with minced vegetables and a rehabilitation regime. And thank God for Barger, as Sandy had said, her green eyes round and sweet. Thank God he was dear enough to buy as many books on rabbit care as Barnes & Noble carried, sweet enough to run to Safeway for cabbage, lovely enough to rub out the tension *being a mother* created in Sandy's neck.

"I remember. Barely," said Barger.

"Do you remember why you named him Wink?" She rolled the sheet in her hands.

"You wouldn't let me name him 'Rest in Peace,'" he said.

"Poor little thing just slept constantly. And his paw! It just broke my heart. Remember what happened to him?"

"Died," he said. He recalled, and perhaps still felt, the sunshine relief that the work was over. It was buried beneath the yellow rosebush at her parents' place. Barger dug the hole and lowered in the shoe box himself. One moment it had been alive and warm in his palm, and in the next moment was a cooling husk. Sandy wept inconsolably most of the day. Barger had lay awake that night, wondering at his own shallow feeling.

Sandy squeezed the sheet in her palm.

"That's not exactly what the dream was," she told him. "I came home from somewhere—work, I guess, because I was dressed in a pants suit—and I found you sitting cross-legged on the floor, feeding Wink from a bottle like he was our baby."

"I can't sit cross-legged," he said. "Hurts my back."

"It was just such a sweet thing, you know? It makes me think of this whole other side of things."

"Where did you work?" he asked. "In the dream, I mean."

Sandy released the sheet. It was wrinkled with the heat of her hands. She adjusted the pillow and lay on her side with her back to him. Turned the lamp off. Barger stiffened and hushed his own breathing, listening for the sobs to rise through the sheets. He'd brought her this far, he thought, had practically explained that they weren't those people they used to be, they had to forget those people, those silly kids they used to be.

"I just thought it was a kind of nice thing," she said.

"Sure. It kind of was."

The first sob came, and then a second—the sound built until inhale and exhale were trying to happen at once. Barger looked at a patch of red light splashed on the wall by the digital clock. A sob shook the bed. He lay still, counting the beats of his heart so he wouldn't lose his temper with her.

Sandy turned over and put her hand flat on his chest. Thank God for him. She lifted herself and in the dark pressed her mouth to his, as if passion, or resuscitation, was what the situation required.

# A SWORD FROM MY COUNTRY

Amelia," he said, his voice a cold track down my spine, though it was summer and the grass smelled burned and I had been looking for shade. I was overdressed for a company picnic, my hair woven into a French braid, a sundress with scooping collar. One of his hands crawled on my shoulder and I could barely say hello. "Let me get a look at you," he said. "Are you still my orchid?"

He stared into my eyes, cracked-gourd smile across his face, and when I looked away I felt him take in the rest of me. I counted to three, then met his stare hard, a trick I'd used on the tenth grade boys who stole looks down my shirt. They turned away, cheeks on fire, but the Major's gaze slid up my throat and brushed my lips before locking with my own.

"That's good cake," he said, pointing at the plate in my hands. "An old Church family recipe. I've been baking most of this last week."

I dragged my plastic fork over the crumbling edge of German chocolate, watched the crumbs scattering across the plate.

"Better if you eat it," he said. I pinched a bite to my tongue, turning my face to him. This time, his eyes cut away. "When you see your father," he said, "tell him I'm looking for him."

"I will, Mr. Church," I said.

I sat alone, cross-legged in the shade of an oak tree, and looked out over the Major's ridiculous backyard, a spectacle of checkerboard tablecloths and ranks of food, men sweating in polo shirts and chinos, their wives keeping one eye on the kids. All of them looked the same to me, little featureless dolls under blonde or red or brunette hair. Not me. My parents adopted me from Vietnam when I was two years old, and though I'm officially an American, my hazel skin and almond eyes tell a different story. I'd come to Church Hardware picnics for as long as I can remember, and only the Major stood out more than me.

Major Church—it was a strange name for such a thin, spectral man. The Major, as everyone called him, would appear in our Sunday newspapers, wearing wings and a halo, to bring the good news of rock-bottom prices. My daddy managed the Caruthers branch of Church Hardware and I suppose he and the Major were something like friends, though I'd seen him imitate his boss, speaking like he'd swallowed steel wool and clasping his hands together in mock prayer. The Major, with his spidery limbs, smiling horse teeth, and sweating skin was easy to make fun of—unless he stood before you. I watched him talking with his branch managers, my father among them, and I saw their measured distance, neither too close nor too far from the Major. They all looked serious, even when it came to tipping back their heads to laugh at his jokes. I shivered again in the heat, mashing up the crumbs of the Church family cake.

"There you are," called my mother. She climbed the small rise where I sat. Her legs were flat and poreless in new panty hose, the grass sawing at her Mary Janes. "What are you doing up here all alone?" She sat down next to me and smoothed her dress over her long legs. Both of us were overdressed. "Your father was summoned to the round table," she said, pointing. "Holding court with the king." She tore up a blade of grass and turned it in her fingers. "The king needs a fool, and lately it's your father." After all the years with Church Hardware, she thought my father should have been managing the Fresno store, the highest paid position in the company next to the Major himself. She had wanted him to wear a tie. "It's a picnic, Sheila," he'd said. "Nobody wears ties at a picky-nick." The drive over had been tense and I was supposed to be keeping her company.

"Are you having a terrific time?" I said.

"Don't get smart." She cut me a sideways look. "Major gets uglier every year, don't you think? By the time he's seventy, he will have turned into an actual mule." She pinched the tender skin behind my arm. Something I hate. "You're still too young to notice those things. Don't be in any rush to start noticing." She cast the blade of grass away, stood up, and brushed down the front of her dress. "I need to go save your father before he says anything stupid," she said. "He's approaching his limit for intelligent speech. Be around."

I watched her sidestep down the hill until she reached my father, laying a hand on his elbow, and then I walked in the opposite direction, toward the koi pond and the swampy overhang of weeping willows. When I was a little girl, I loved this backyard with its sprawling lawn and hidden corners, lookouts, surprises. I would run with the other children, my dress lifting like wings and showing the world my canary panties. But the others had outgrown coming or their dads had found other jobs, and I was the only fifteen-year-old, stuck between grade school games of tag and the dull business of adults.

I watched the fish cut swift lines in the motionless water and my reflection peered back. Koi swam through my eyes, in and out my ears, breeched my mouth. When I pictured what my life would have been like in Vietnam, if I'd never been adopted, this is what I see: my face rippled in the water, flat sky above, empty country on all sides.

Daddy and the Major sat with their chairs huddled together. My mother smoked a cigarette and faced away from the scrum. She hadn't smoked in three months and looked odd, unpracticed, more than guilty. I sat with my back to her, crossing my legs under my dress. I felt her fingers working to unbraid my hair, her nervous habit since I was little, but I slid from her reach, closer to Daddy.

The Major said, "I hope you fired her, Gene. She was stealing, right? You know me, I don't like to push myself on my managers, but theft is theft."

Daddy was nodding. "That's definitely true. But she was taking stuff for her son's science fair project. She promised to pay every cent back and even gave me five bucks on the spot. I figured, what the hell, you know, no harm, no foul."

The Major's long face turned to me, softened. He leaned back in his chair and smiled. Daddy picked his teeth and scanned across the picnic. "Gene, you didn't tell me Amelia had turned into a young lady. Last time I saw her, she was in pigtails."

"She's growing," he said.

"Like a weed," my mother added. "She'll be driving soon."

I flattened my hands on the cool grass, keeping them from plucking it up blade by blade. The Major's tongue moved against the back of his teeth like a fish. I didn't know his age, but I'd always thought him ancient, eternally old and excessively rich.

"Excuse me," he said, rising to his full height, still looking down on me. I refused to squirm under his stare.

As soon as he was out of earshot, my mother turned to Daddy. "You told me you were going to fire that woman."

"What could I do, Sheila? We don't pay her enough."

"He's the one who needs to hear it."

"You don't tell your boss he's a cheapskate."

"No, *you* tell your boss that you're harboring thieves."

"Jesus H. Christ," he said. "Can't I even have a business conversation?"

"Obviously not."

Mom took another cigarette from her silver case.

"What about that smoke?" he said. "You promised us."

"Don't you dare lecture me." She lifted the lighter to her mouth, hands shaking. It clicked once, twice. "Damn," she said, throwing the cigarette unlit into the lawn. She pressed her hand to the bridge of her nose, shut her eyes. "Get me out of here, Gene, or I swear I'll get myself out." She grabbed my shoulder before Daddy could say anything. "Go get my purse, honey, my black one. It's in the guest room."

I crossed the lawn to the Major's enormous house. The lower windows were open, rooms displayed, some occupied by guests, but the second story glass was pale with the backs of curtains. Looking back at my parents, they seemed soft and in love, mouths and hands almost touching, but I knew the whispers raging between them.

I reached the veranda door and went inside. The air was cooler, ceiling fans spinning overhead. A long, white couch faced me and a television flashed light onto the cushions. I heard squalls of the picnic receding behind me, but the was house quiet and empty, another world. Letting my hair out of its braid, I combed my fingers through tangles, the day's pent-up heat leaving my scalp. I decided the Major's house suited him, wide-open spaces for his rambling shape.

The guestroom was just down the hall, but I climbed the stairs instead, wanting to lose myself in this expanse of quiet. Open doors squared in the hallway and I looked into each one: a plain spare bedroom, a sewing room wallpapered with butterflies, an elegant tiled bath, another bedroom as stark as the first. So much space unfilled. But the last door was closed. I tried the knob and pushed it open, knew at once it was different.

The Major's study was dim. The walls were covered with framed newspaper clippings, certificates with embossed medallions and gold borders, and a color picture of the Major in his angel costume. No sale or appliance was being advertised—just a thin man dressed in soft, billowy white, his skeletal hands making a steeple before his chest, heaven in his eyes.

His desk was in the middle of the room, facing the door, its top clean except for a calendar and five hardcovers, propped between bookends forged with the letters *M* and *C*. I settled into his chair and spun a few times before opening the drawers. Behind a sheaf of manila folders, I found a wooden box engraved with Vietnamese figures, deep gouges, but meticulously patterned. Running my fingers through the symbols, I felt the whittled roughness left by the knife, wishing I could read my own language. I opened the hasp. A photograph lay face down and I turned it to see a face not so different from my own, a girl a few years older than me, leaning close to the soldier at her side. She seemed like a piece of the landscape, as if the boy had gotten himself photographed next to a pretty sign. His mouth was laughing wide while hers rested in a wan, silent smile. Where she was delicate, small-boned, soft, he looked cut, sharpened, his thinness a danger. It took me a moment, but I recognized the soldier. He would trade his Army fatigues for wings and a halo.

"I called her Fran," said the Major.

I jumped at his voice and he took the photograph from my hand. He stood between the doorway and me. He cupped the picture in his palm so the image of her curved toward him. "Don't you think she was pretty? She lived in a village we liberated," he said. His eyes lifted to me. "Lived in a hut smaller than this room. With two grandparents, a mother, about ten chickens, and two dogs. Her father was probably trying to kill us, and I don't know which, the chickens or the dogs, were meant for the oven." He ended with a laugh that brought heat into the room. "Do they talk about the war in school?"

I shrugged.

"I wasn't one of the bad ones," he said. "I wasn't there to rape the country." He replaced the picture, closed the box, put it carefully back in the drawer. The smile he gave me was the same one he wore with his angel costume.

"Let me show you something more interesting," he said.

He slid back the closet door and lifted out a green canvas bag with stenciled black numbers. He pulled open the drawstrings and the smell of ancient sweat and mothballs hit me. He withdrew a sword. The scabbard was black and decorated with silver swirls of flowers and vines, curving elegantly and ending in a metal thimble. The handle looked made of ivory, white with a deep, black grain, capped with the head of a snarling lion. It's tongue hissed between its teeth and curled around to meet the blade. "This is a sword from your country. I never made major," he said. "Isn't that funny? I only made corporal. My buddies used to call me Major Corporal and salute." He held the sword in his palms as if it possessed the magic to hover between us. "Bought this in Saigon from a little old man selling trinkets on the roadside, mostly junk, bicycle wheels and dented tin mugs. He almost didn't sell it to me."

He turned it in his fingers, showing me every angle. The room had become thick with the Major's cologne.

He took the handle in one hand, the scabbard in the other, and unsheathed it. The blade flashed. He waved it, eyes moving with the sword's slow dance, reading a message in its steel that I couldn't see or understand. He fell into a half-crouch, all his weight in his bent knees, stepping to the balls of his feet, smoothing the air between us.

The sound was unlike anything I'd heard. Musical, but not a song—not a scream or a prayer. I closed my eyes and could feel it churning a few feet away, like standing on a ledge with the entire world blowing up at me.

He whispered, "Hold out your hand."

I reached out with two fists.

"No, like this." He turned my wrists and unfolded my fingers, then placed the flat of the blade in my palms. The sword wasn't heavy, yet felt solid, dense, as if there was more to it than engraved metal. It wasn't cold the way steel is cold—it was cold the way a grape leaf is cold, the trunk of a tree is cold.

"Hold out one finger." On the last joint he placed the flat of the blade. "Perfectly balanced," he said.

As it swayed there I pretended to read the engravings through my skin, imagining what a sword like this might say to a girl balancing a piece of Vietnam as far from her body as possible, at the very edge of her being.

My fingers snaked around the handle. I could feel speed in the edge of the blade, a weight that would jump in any direction my hands led it. I moved my wrists, the blade followed, impossible to go ungracefully.

"Hold it straight up," he said. "Think balance. Draw into your body. Raise your hands. Let the blade fall almost to your shoulder. Be in control, be balanced. Hold it there. Let it hover. Do you feel it?"

"Yes," I whispered.

"Levitate. Let the weight of the hilt do the work. Breathe. Be in control of your breath."

I filled my lungs, exhaled, felt my pulse in my hands. The blade floated above my sleeve, away from my ear. My eyes closed and I could hear the tidal roar of steel.

"When you're ready, when you feel in command, bring the sword down to the left, slashing down. Be aware of your body, your feet. Know where you are in the world. Don't let go until you're ready."

I waited for the sword to work through my hands.

The swing ignited, the blade followed, cutting out its place.

The tip of the sword floated a breath from the floor, and as soon as I saw it in my hands it became too heavy for me to hold. The point fell first and the hilt met the ground with a crash.

My vision churned with spots. "I'm sorry," I said.

"No." His voice sang and he stepped toward me. He knelt, limbs all protruding corners, eyes burning with a blue flame. He reached toward me and his hand trembled. His fingertip traced my cheek, scratched across my lips.

"Mr. Church—"

"Hush," he said. A tinny laughter whistled from him. "Christ, I was only there three years. It was a lifetime ago." I held my breath as his palm lay down flat over my chest, my pounding heart, trembling. I wanted to back away but was held, somehow, by his open hand. His voice at a crescendo whisper said, "You are my orchid."

The room flooded with light and I felt someone standing behind me. The Major's hand snapped back. He brushed his face but his mouth was twisted in a smile he couldn't scrape off, tall teeth and thin, bloodless lips.

I turned around, and there was my mother. Silence stretched.

"Come on, it wasn't that, Sheila," said the Major. "How long have you known me? Look," he said, picking up the sword and holding it to me, as if the offering would explain everything. "It's from Vietnam," he said.

"I'll see you rot," she hissed, grabbing my wrist and pulling me from the room. I stumbled to keep up, fell, but she dragged me to my feet again and we were outside, cutting through the party to my father. "What about your purse," I kept saying, but she pulled me to the car, opened the door, loaded me. She caught my face between her hands and looked so hard into my eyes that I went silent.

"What did that man do to you?" she said. "What did he do?"

My father stood next to her, bewildered.

"Take us home, Gene," she said, slamming my door. Through the car window I saw her face draw close to his ear. I expected her to cry, but when she turned to me, she steeled. Not a crack showed in her skin. I saw myself change in her eyes, become something I wasn't.

Daddy slipped in behind the wheel, my mother next to him. She rode close to him, their shoulders almost touching. He wouldn't look at me, not even flick his gaze to the rearview mirror, but she turned around and glared. Her stare covered me as if reading a confession. "You're going to tell me what happened in that room."

"Nothing," I said. I looked at my father's silent shape, at the neighborhood rushing by, all manicured trees and dormant chimneys, no fires. "He was just—*you* don't understand," I said. "That sword came from my country."

"*This* is your country, Amelia. *We* are your parents."

"Didn't you see Vietnam once? When you adopted me. You've never told me anything about it."

"Amelia—"

"What did it look like? How did they live there?" My mother's face slipped into blankness. She saw me, her daughter, her Amelia, but didn't recognize me. Her eyes danced with mine and we were strangers. "How come you won't tell me anything?" I said. "Are you scared I'll run back there?"

My father growled, "If you want to see Vietnam, I'll buy you a map. Books. Anything you want. I've got a good job, you know." He turned to my mother and, as if I'd vanished, said, "This is what I meant, Sheila. You have to be able to trust some people. You have to."

"Leave it alone, Gene," said my mother.

I wanted to stare them down, let my parents see what strength I could summon. I made a loose fist and could almost feel the rough of the handle, the weight of steel.

We lurched into our driveway. In one motion my father killed the engine and opened his door. He turned, said to both of us, "Maybe if you hadn't dressed her like a Saigon whore."

The car door slammed. My mother's chin pressed forward, jaw firm and straight, lips together in a flat smile. She touched my hair, curled a rope around her finger, held tight. "Don't listen to that talk, he's—Amelia, you've got to tell me what happened."

I said, "I don't know."

# GRANDEUR

*for Charles Bukowski*

It all happened that summer of West Nile virus, when the news put sick people on TV and ran stories on how mosquito repellent was flying off the Wal-Mart shelves. I had a job trolling the streets of Fresno bagging and tagging dead birds. We believed that the virus would manifest itself in birds first, that they were predictors of how the sickness would move through humankind, and that summer the birds were falling from their perches in the trees and probably right out of their flight patterns. I had a government-issue phone, and I'd be sent on calls to pick a bird out of someone's pool. They float—I think I'm one of few people who'd know that—and I'd use my government skimmer to take them off the top. Then dead birds became such a common sight people stopped making reports. I'd be driving home and see them littering the highway like a load spilled off a truck. I blocked traffic bagging and tagging, horns blasting behind me, cars backed up for miles. I was called names, considered crazy. Me, the fine line separating public health from an epidemic, called crazy.

"I know how you feel," my researcher friend Henry told me, after I complained to him about my circumstances. He always came outside to smoke an unfiltered with me after I dropped off my specimens. This particular day he had a pink smear of bird blood in the shape of a talon on his smock, as if one of the avian cadavers had fought back. He pushed his glasses up his nose. He was constantly pushing his glasses up his nose. We were both sweating in the summer heat—Henry worse because he was used to the air conditioning inside the lab. He dropped his smoke in the alley and smothered it with his shoe. His caterpillar eyebrows were visible over the rims of his glasses: the specs were on their way down his nose again. He said, "You should take your missus along with you tomorrow. Get her out of the house."

"A date with the reaper," I said.

"Don't flatter yourself, Pet. At most you're his janitor."

"Speaking of," I said, walking around the pickup, jangling my keys.

"Why don't you take the rest of the day," Henry said, talking as if he had the authority to grant vacations. "Go home, have a nice meal, wine and dine the lady."

"You're the boss," I told him, and drove away.

Actually, I was heading home. I had been heading home for three days now. I *wanted* to go home. The missus and I leased in a northeast neighborhood, our house was only a few years old, its closets still smelled like new carpet. A grand place from what I remembered. I thought I could rest there. And I was on my way home again when I saw the black bullets of dead crows under a streetlight. I pulled over to the curb only a few blocks from my house, telling myself I was seeing things, I needed to go home and rest. Then I heard the muffled thump of another one hitting the pavement, then another, and then they really started falling, a hailstorm. I watched them splatter. They lay prone on their backs, feet up, wings out, or on their shoulders with their backs to me, elongated, elegant black.

I should have gone home anyway. I was all set to do exactly that, to restart the engine and drive away, when I saw him. He was skipping from the circular glow of one streetlamp to another, like a kid doing puddles. He had an umbrella and a white dust mask. I watched him squat before a crow and prod it with something. We called his type *novitiates*, regular citizens who tried to examine the dead birds without our equipment or training—novitiates suffered delusions, and were known to have a death wish. They were considered somewhere between a nuisance and a threat to public health, and it was official policy to prevent a novitiate from contaminating a sample. Instead of continuing home, I got out of the truck and approached the scene. Once I'd gotten closer, I saw that he was poking the crow with a ballpoint pen. He looked up at me, startled, the dust mask practically glowing. "You must be with the CDC," he shouted, his voice muffled.

Close enough, I thought.

"It's the plague of crows over here." He toured me around the corpses, holding the umbrella over us. There were four dozen at first count, black humps of fresh crow. They lay in the street, guttered up next to the curb, on the sidewalks and grass strips. When I went over the area with my flashlight I found more on roofs, stuck in rain gutters or nested up against chimneys. The novitiate felt the need to explain the relationship between death and falling. "The real question is cause or effect," he said. "If they died in the air, then hit the ground, or if they hit the ground while still alive."

I didn't say much. Bag and tag.

"It's West Nile, isn't it? It's started right here in my neighborhood."

"The birds have to be autopsied first."

"Oh, I already know what will happen," he said, smoothing a few wiry strands to his bald crown, looking into the night over the rim of his mask. "These will go into some lab but no answers will ever come out."

"No news is good news."

"People already have *news*," he said. "We want Information. We want to be informed."

"I can understand that," I said.

"It starts with you, you know. What can you tell me about these specimens?"

"Well, they're dead. But I guess you told me that."

"Is it official policy to make fun of the citizenry?"

"No, sir," I said.

"I pay taxes. I vote in every election at every level. I fill out my census immediately. I have a right to know what's happening right here in my own backyard."

"I can't tell you much," I said. "But crows are never a good sign."

"I thought not," he said, nodding but looking scared. His skin was going as pale as the dust mask, the blood draining out of his face.

"They're big birds, you know. It takes a lot to bring one down. This many?" I shrugged my shoulders, letting him fill in the blank with the terrible truth. I said, "Have you been out here long, sir?"

"I—a half hour, I'd guess."

"And you've been wearing that mask the whole time, correct?"

"Oh, God—"

"—You're a wise man to have kept that mask on."

For a second I thought he was going to collapse and weep in the street. "What about you?" he asked, the fear in his voice cutting right through the mask. "You're... unprotected."

I stopped my work to give him a meaningful look. I leaned in a little closer. I could smell the breath leaking out—as if that cup of paper could stop a dread disease, it couldn't even stop halitosis. "There's a government vaccine," I said.

He recoiled a step. "I knew it."

"Excuse me," I said, and turned to my job, leaving him to think he'd been right all along, the best feeling any of us can have.

Each bird got its own bag, with a tag relating the location I found it, and whether in fresh, desiccated, or decomposed condition. The fresh ones went straight to the researchers' tables. I marked the spot I found them with Xs of pink spray paint, so if they found West Nile in the bird they could search the area scientifically. Such cases—clustered specimens, we called them—created a lot of excitement in the lab. I always called ahead. The boys and girls in goggles would be waiting on the curb for my truck to pull up, filled with bumpy, orange bags. *Enough for everybody*, I would joke with them. The imminence of disease spreading through the air turned us on. Our careers—our lives—had meaning, hard work and dedication about to be recognized.

It was certainly the granddaddy of clustered specimens but I got them all. Into hedges to retrieve birds, up onto roofs, an arm's reach down a chimney, where a crow had come to rest in an abandoned barn owl nest. I left pink Xs on box shrubs and composite shingles and bricks. I ended up having to finish with an audience of morning commuters leaving their homes for work, which of course was not ideal. No one is friendly finding you on his roof. They were less than understanding about the Xs, calling it defacement, calling it *criminal*. One day soon, I thought, they'd look back and be glad I was there. The man who cut West Nile off at the pass, who put public health above the petty concerns of property damage and trespassing—they'd talk about me with reverence for years to come, the hero of the West Nile story.

I tooted my horn when I pulled into the alley behind the lab. I had a feeling this was the one that would prove all our fears and it came from practically my own neighborhood. I watched in the rearview while the researchers unloaded the birds, two orange bags for each smock, like hunting trophies or harvest bounty, our reasons for being. Henry knocked on the passenger window and held up his pack of smokes and a Zippo. I shut off the engine. "I figured you'd have been home by now," I said, getting out of the cab.

"Who among us goes home?" Henry passed me a lit cigarette. The paper was moist from his lips. "I thought you went home as well, and look at us, both right here."

"Touché," I said.

The floor of the alley was still in shade, cool from the night, but a blade of sunlight was working its way down the lab wall like a slow-moving guillotine. Henry and I watched its progress awhile without talking. Then I started telling him about the specimens. He lit me another cig as I talked.

"So this is the batch, for sure," he said.

"That's what I figured."

"She's arrived, my friend. The ship's come in."

"Armageddon is upon us," I said.

He tossed away his cigarette and pushed up his glasses just in time. "It'll be more like a thinning out," he said. "The frail and elderly first. Then the indigent."

"We'll save the rest," I said.

"That's the spirit, Pet." He slapped my back. "We've got to be patient. It'll all be worth it in the end."

Patience, I kept thinking while driving home. I was learning how to be patient with a disease that refused to make its grand entrance. I asked Henry to call me on the official phone the minute they found something—I insisted he call me—but I couldn't help thinking that one of the lab boys, perhaps the very second I drove away, was calling out, "Eureka!" and they'd proudly celebrate the discovery of life's destruction without me. Could I count on Henry to interrupt the orgy and say, "That's one of Pet's, Pet brought that bird in, let me give him a ring and we can all toast Pet?!" I depended so much on the birds and the clues their deaths contained. Without them, I was just a trash man. The birds made me a hero on the frontlines.

———o

In the living room of my house a woman was asleep on my couch, wearing panties and a T-shirt, one leg slung over the back. Her chipped, painted toenails looked like tiny dishes. I stood there blinking at her. Her name was Camille. We were married. I decided the best thing was not to wake her. Let her finish her sleep. I'd get breakfast ready, and then she could explain to me why she was sleeping on the couch. Except I was noisy in the kitchen. Clanger of bowls, dropper of eggs, shouter of curses. I went out for some fresh air instead.

Our paper lay wrapped in a plastic sleeve on the lawn. I checked the mailbox but the postal woman hadn't been by yet. I sat on the porch with the *Fresno Bee* and turned through the sections looking for another picture of myself. About six months before I'd appeared on the front page, just doing my job. Today there wasn't anything worthwhile. I folded it up and let it balance on my thigh. I sat there squinting out at the warm morning, the familiar houses, the cars in the driveways and at the curbs. The image symbolized for me what I'd been doing out there for three days straight: Protecting everyone's right to come home at night and stay until morning. I—we, my cohorts and I—braved the worst scenarios so no one else had to.

It was so quiet and still. I watched down the block for a door to open, a car to back into the street and drive away, a school bus to come around a corner and load up some kids. I strained to hear something besides the lazy knock of oak branches against my roof, or the sea-sounding breeze in the fig leaves. I looked again at the newspaper:

Was that date really today? Had something happened I wasn't aware of, stopping time? Had Henry let me down? Then, entering my senses as if surfacing for breath, I heard the scratching, so soft I thought it might be a product of my imagination. I sat perfectly still and waited. I heard it again. Like the tearing of paper. Like the whittling down of wood by sharp knives. Like clawing-out. Goose-fleshed, I tried to discern the source. I scanned the street from one horizon to the other before I realized the scratching was coming from behind me, within my own house.

I burst through the front door. Camille was at the sink and I startled her. She glared at me wide-eyed, her hair a tangled nest from the couch. "What the hell, Pet—"

"—Sshh!" I crawled alongside the wall, listening. "You hear that?" I whispered.

"All I hear is the thin ice cracking under your feet."

"Sshh!" The sound had leaped into a frenzy and then fallen silent. I'd heard that before. I knew then what I had inside the wall. "It's birds," I told Camille.

"Of course it is."

"Somehow we've got birds trapped in the wall."

I looked up and down the textured surface, decorated with pictures. Occasions, family. I hardly recognized my face in any of them. Crawling left and right, I rapped with my fist, listening with my ear near the baseboard for a response.

"This is too much," Camille said.

"I'm trying to listen."

"Bullshit, Pet. Bull. Shit. You're crawling around like a nutcase, that's what you're doing."

"Here," I said. I'd heard their answer despite the distraction in the room. I scratched a mark into the paint with my thumbnail then went to get my tape measure, then took the measurement from the front door to the spot.

"I want you to leave whatever it is alone and talk to me," Camille told me. "I want whatever it is to stop. Okay? You can't keep staying gone, Pet. It worries me sick and I can't take it anymore."

She stood there with her arms crossed over her chest, her bare thighs touching under the T-shirt hem, and her face was red and swollen with tears. She was waiting for me to tell her that everything was fine but I didn't know yet. I had a job to do.

"Tell me where you've been!"

"Just a second."

"Who is she? Tell me who she is!"

I went out to the porch again. Pages of the newspaper were plastered against the spindles by the breeze. Pieces of it tumbled over our lawn into our neighbor's. I measured from the front door and painted a pink X where the birds were entombed.

Camille stood in the doorway. "What in fuck are you doing?"

"Marking the location."

She seemed to see me in a different light then. Her head cocked a little to one side and her eyes, which had been stained with tears, now shone with understanding. Her voice came soft and musical. "Who can I call, Pet? Tell me a name. There must be someone I can call for help."

"This is my job, honey. I do this every day."

I retrieved my reciprocating saw from the garage, and when I came back, Camille was leaning on the porch rail with her back to the world. Gooseflesh stood alert on her thighs. Her bare feet had left moist footprints on the boards where she'd been pacing. "Let me call someone," she said.

"I am the one people call," I assured her.

If she said something in response the buzz of the saw covered it up. I pushed the blade into the siding, cutting out a square panel to free the birds—working from outside so I wouldn't release the virus into our living room, for Camille's sake. The story swelled in my head to grand proportions: *Hero bird collector finds disease in own house, saves all.*

I removed the cut siding. A talus slope of hollow bones poured out, a burial ground of my avian friends. "Look at that," I said, full of wonder. Somehow the bones had been speaking to me.

But I, Pet Petersen, was talking to no one. Camille had gone inside. I got an orange bag from my truck. I poured handfuls of the bones into the sack. I wrote down my address, then marked the box *desiccated.*

No one came out of the lab when I blew the horn. I banged and banged on the door, and a researcher I didn't know finally opened up. "What in the world is it?" he asked me.

I held out the bag. The bones rattled together like chips of ice when he took it. He regarded me, then peeked inside the sack, a violation of safety regulations. Slowly his eyes lifted to mine. I said, "Henry here?"

"He went home," the researcher said.

"What happened? Did you find West Nile?"

He shook his head no. "It's been a frustrating day," he said, then started to slide away from me into the lab. "Maybe this one," he said sarcastically, rattling the sack of bones.

"They came from my house," I said.

He nodded once and shut the door. I heard the deadbolt engage as per regulations, though it felt personal.

I sat in the truck with the AC going full blast until it smelled musty and was blowing lukewarm air. I could barely breathe. There was this painful speed to my heart. It was beating the back of my breastbone as if to get out, and all at once I understood what was going on inside me. It explained why I couldn't get home, why I found specimens everywhere I went, why I heard them in my wall. I put my hand on my chest. I knew all about birds—I'd been highly trained by the government—but still I wasn't prepared to feel one in there, where a heart should be.

It wasn't fair. Instead of being on the cover of *Time*, this development would put me in the tabloids. People would only read about my life while waiting to pay for groceries. All the good deeds I'd done would be blown away by the turbulence of a bird in my chest.

I worked hard to catch my breath. I did my best to arrange a natural face, even checking my color in the truck's chrome bumper. Henry would have known something was wrong with me, but Henry had abandoned the cause. I knocked and knocked on the lab door. The same researcher opened up, and I wondered if he was in there by himself. "What's your problem, guy?" he said.

"I need to borrow a scalpel," I said. He looked at me over his perfectly fitting glasses. I missed Henry. Henry I could have told exactly what was going on inside me. Henry would have lit me a smoke and heard me. I told this other guy, "I just got a report of clustered specimens in a vineyard outside of town and I need a scalpel."

"What for?"

I huffed impatiently, talking fast to cover up how my voice trembled. "You ever been to a clustered specimen site in a vineyard? Fucking mayhem, man. The canes—that's what they call the branch of a grapevine, cane, as in *hell*—just about swallow a bird whole. It's like surgery getting them out. Hence—" I held out my hand.

He regarded me once more then went inside. He left the door standing open, and I could see my bird bones being classified on a metal table. They looked yellow in contrast to the stainless steel. We'd find no answers in those bones, I guessed, and the bird in my ribs started flying loops as if to tell me my guess was right. Then the researcher was back, holding a scalpel to me handle first.

"You loan this blade in service to your fellow man," I said.

"Whatever," he said, shutting and bolting the lab door in my face.

Most days I would have thought about reporting his multiple safety violations, or dwelt on his rudeness, but today I wasn't in a petty mood. Driving home, my bird-heart was expanding to see the beauty in all things. The ripples of heat on the road ahead of me like the ocean. The brake lights flashing on and off in traffic as if choreographed. The palpitations of a doomed man.

I got home and found my own door unlocked, yet another violation of safety rules. I stepped inside and knew at once that Camille had left me. There were no signs, per se, just a tremendous emptiness that one feels when stepping into a deserted house. But of course it didn't matter. Actually I was glad she wouldn't have to witness what was coming next.

I'd brought an orange bag inside with me. I went upstairs and turned on the bathroom tap and took off my shirt. Looking at myself in the mirror, at the distinct tan lines ending at my neck and biceps, at the scalpel in my hand. I cut the air over my chest, trying to visualize the incisions that would get the bird out. My reflection blurred through the tears in my eyes. I breathed deep, telling myself I had to, for the sake of humankind. But how unfortunate that my every good deed be eclipsed for the sake of a lost bird.

I opened the window for fresh air, and as I stood there looking out over the tops of the young trees in our neighborhood my bird heart leaped with joy. The greenery washed back and forth in the breeze like foam on a sea, and I was led out the window to squat at the edge of my roof, my toes in the rain gutter, my hands folded up close to my body. What a pretty world we've made, so full of perches, growing toward the sky. And what a shame that it's all going to come tumbling down.

# ACKNOWLEDGMENTS

I wish to express my gratitude to the editors of the publications in which these stories first appeared: "Ain't it Pretty" in *StringTown*; "The Atlas Show" in *Slow Trains*; "The Rules" in *Prick of the Spindle*; "Retreat" in *Writers' Dojo*; "A Sword from my Country" in *Eclectica*; "Brother Rhino" in *Pine Grove Literary Review*; "Candelario" in *Nailed*; "Grandeur" in *Prime Number*.

For reading early, often unrecognizable versions of these stories, thanks to Pete Fromm, Jack Driscoll, Carly Furry, Brad Fritsch, Samantha Self, Darlene Pagán, Brent Johnson, and Kyle Lang. To Alissa Nielsen, for offering insightful comment on the final manuscript, I owe a debt I won't soon be able to repay. For the team at sunnyoutside, Brian Mihok and David McNamara, I have much respect and fondness. If it weren't for Katey Schultz's infectious enthusiasms in the pursuit of writing, I'd have given up my own pursuit long ago. And if it weren't for the support Trish and Sam Walker, I'd have no reason to keep going.

# AUTHOR'S BIO

John Carr Walker's stories have been appearing in literary journals since 2007. He's the founder of *Trachodon Magazine* and a 2012 Fishtrap Fellow. A native of California's San Joaquin Valley and former high school teacher, he now lives and writes full-time in Saint Helens, Oregon.